Jeffrey Cook

Street Fair

Book Two of the Fair Folk Chronicles
by Jeffrey Cook and Katherine Perkins

Cover by Clarissa Yeo of Yocla Designs
Text Copyright © 2016 Jeffrey Cook and Katherine Perkins
This is a work of fiction. Names, characters, businesses, places,
and events are either imaginary or used in a fictitious manner.
All Rights Reserved

Dedicated to Mr. William Shakespeare,
from whom we cannot seem to get away.

Table of Contents

Chapter 1: Evaluation

"Conflict in Gaelic Cultures is a 400-level course, Mr. Thomas. They knew it was going to be difficult when they signed up." Dr. Brian O'Neill paused just long enough to let the other voice on the phone utter two and a half sentences before interrupting. "Do any of them discuss all nine salient points covered in class?" This time the pause was only for two and a half syllables before he interrupted his TA again. "Then no one earned an A. I don't think the instructions could be any clearer."

He allowed a few more words as he walked briskly through the mostly empty halls, then continued, speaking just as briskly. "All the more so for the first test of the Summer quarter. A bit of tactical advice, Mr. Thomas: always set the bar clearly high from the beginning of the term, when they still have time to do better quality work." He began the first of three flights of stairs, his free hand clutching the duffle bag over his shoulder to keep it from jostling irritatingly. "And their electing to take the class in what could have been a vacation term is commendable, but it does not change the grading standards of the university."

He was intent on not letting his breathing get too much heavier as he spoke. "I'm sure you'll handle those questions ably in your own office hours. Mine will not resume until the Autumn. My current research is very time-consuming. I'll see you Monday." He hung up as he reached the third flight of stairs, then the final hallway.

Dr. O'Neill reached his office. He took a deep breath, whispered a few syllables in an old dialect of Gaelic, and shifted his foot in one shoe a little to make sure the penny he'd placed in the heel was still there, even if he'd been vaguely aware of it throughout the long walk. Caution was critical. Finally, he reached for the doorknob, turned — then paused, looking about to make sure he was actually alone, before he slipped into his office.

As he closed the door, he checked to make sure the horseshoe was still nailed perfectly above it. Over the window, he'd gone with daisy chains to complement the salt on the windowsill.

He set the filthy duffle bag on the desk and opened it, removing stack after stack of damp $20 bills. His thumb brushed off some of the grime from the top bill of each stack.

He lifted one closer in the florescent light. "L-7-2..." His voice rang clear, even when just reading a serial number. "525..." Precision was important—so, so important—but it wasn't everything. "383..." He should be able to command attention if he were reading the phone book. "...B. Exactly so. For the first."

Then he replaced the bills in the bag, set it down, and took his seat at his desk.

Fifteen centuries of genealogy charts, on various qualities of paper and various things that technically were not paper at all, covered the left wall of the office. He glanced over at them, studying name after name. He looked at one of the lowest ones, printed out in a calligraphic font on multipurpose laser paper: *Brian Angus Ui Niall.*

He refocused. He opened drawers, taking out antique coins from one and an old book from another. He laid the coins out on his desk and stared a while, then carefully perused a few pages of the book. Frowning, he put the coins away. He rose and stepped over to the right wall of his office. Taking down a framed certificate, he studied it for a few moments as he returned to his seat.

This is to certify that BRIAN ANGUS O'NEILL, having submitted a thesis entitled The Wielding of Sacred Power in Ancient Ireland *and having satisfied all the conditions prescribed by the Statutes of the University, was on 1 June 2002 admitted to the degree of DOCTOR OF PHILOSOPHY.*

Very slowly, he took apart the frame and ran his fingers over the certificate—over the historic seal, the name, the title—with a look of regret. He stared for a while at the left wall. He took a deep breath, put the certificate into a folder, and put the folder in the book.

The resulting melancholy of the room was broken by an inordinately chipper voice. "Did you remember to check that the bills were 1969A? You try to pass on knockoffs to people like this, and…Well, actually, I'd love to see that. Don't check."

Dr. O'Neill nearly knocked over his chair as he scrambled up. "But … *how?*"

The boyish figure standing there, shaking out a shaggy mane of tawny hair, smiled too big. "The daisy chains are a nice touch, but you need some along the floorboards. You've got a mouse-hole behind the mini-fridge. So, what about my retainer?"

Having regained his composure—pointedly so—Dr. O'Neill strode over and opened said mini-fridge. He removed a tall, frosty glass of milk and handed it over. Then he ventured, "Not to inquire too much, Rob, but isn't a glass of milk for a retainer in keeping with brownie protocols?"

"Them, certain dime-novel detectives, mice who also want cookies, ultraviolent dystopian thugs—don't even try to label me, Doc. I can go from milk to a nice Chianti in nothing flat."

"Noted." Dr. O'Neill, attempting to be ever so casual, also checked the bag of $20 bills once more, to make sure the year was right.

"Of course it is. So how's the master plan going?"

"Well enough. I'll let you know when I need you. The first part's just going to be coordination, finding the nexus point, making the initial deals, setting out, and..." He trailed off, before trying to smoothly trail into another sentence entirely. "And it doesn't trouble you?" He picked something off a far corner of his desk. "What I've done? What I may do?"

'That's just it, oh Captain, my Captain, or ..." Rob took a look at the left wall of the room, then gave him a mocking bow. "...whatever it will be. What you're doing will trouble everyone. And that's more fun." He smiled, again too big. "Why do you ask, Doc? Do you think I'm scared of what you chipped off of old gates?" He stepped closer than any concept of personal space—and closer than someone fidgeting with slivers of wrought iron might expect. "Do you think I'll stab you in the back?"

"Rob, buddy," Dr. O'Neill spread his arms as much as possible while being careful with what he was holding. "No need to worry at all." He met the yellow eyes evenly. "I *know* you're going to stab me in the back. Just not yet."

Rob stepped back, still smiling. "That's why you're the smart guy. Remember, though, you're calling in a solid, not a guided tour. I'll be a distraction when you need it, but I'm not going to hold your hand. Making sure people *don't* get lost isn't any of my schticks."

Dr. O'Neill nodded. "Provided I get all the information I need, triangulating the locations should not be a problem," he said as he looked to examine the tiny scraps of wing-membrane pinned to the butterfly board.

Chapter 2: Summer Plans

"Guess what's coming to town this weekend?" Lani asked, once they'd settled into the booth at the burger joint after placing their orders at the counter. Megan, Lani, and Justin no longer had to limit themselves to the park within walking distance, ever since Lani and her father had finished working on her car.

Megan spread her hands slightly. "If it's another opportunity to get your picture taken with Grant Imahara, I want to point out that I already did my part helping you the first time."

"No, no, that picture is still perfectly framed on my desk, thank you. This is bigger. You know the Fremont Solstice Fair?"

"Tales of naked bicyclists are hard to miss. Cassia's band is playing it this year, aren't they?"

"Yes, and also this year, there's going to be a path to the Goblin Market!"

Megan raised an eyebrow. "And that would be...?"

Lani was still bouncing with excitement on her side of the booth. "Well, obviously, there's some tricky fourth-dimensional stuff—"

"Obviously," said Megan.

"—which is part of the reason they only put out so many carefully-selected paths for each event. Last time they were sort of close, Mom thought I was too little. Even this year, she said we had to wait until school was out to talk about it. But she says I can go, and I can take you."

"Which is great and all, and I get that you're excited. But what is it?"

"Okay, well, it's sort of like a fair..."

"Does it have naked bicyclists and cotton candy too?" Megan asked, amused.

"Those might be some of the more mundane things there, sure. But there's not really any comparison between it and anything you'll find here. It's, well... it's a faerie fair."

"And you want to go?"

"So do you. If nothing else, just for the magical artwork."

"There'll be magical artwork?" Megan asked, suddenly more intrigued.

"Thought that might catch your attention. Paintings that move, ancient statues, books from the Library of Alexandria, working golems, you name it. Artist's row stretches for miles."

"I've had enough golems, but the rest sounds interesting."

"Okay, so no iron golems. That wouldn't go over well. But, think of it like a carnival, bazaar, and magical strip mall rolled into one, covering about five miles in all directions, and operating in a sort of timelessness, so that as far as the mortal world goes, you step into and out of the path without going anywhere. You can go in and out like that for a few of our days, and then they pack up and take their temporal anomaly with them."

"Seriously? It just vanishes?"

"That's how the Goblin Market works, yes. No one knows where they go between events. But while it's there, you can find anything."

"Except iron golems." Megan noted, with a grin.

"Yes, smartass, fine. Everything except iron golems. "

"All right, so they have everything, and we can check out artist's row. It sounds like fun."

"Okay, but we need to take Justin with us..." Lani exchanged nods with Justin as he looked up very briefly from perusing the menu. "And Ashling. And we need to be really careful."

"Well, of course Justin is coming with us," Megan said. She grinned, just a little sheepishly, at the quiet boy, who as usual was stalwartly sitting between Megan and passersby. "And it's Faerie stuff. We always need to be careful."

"Okay, like, extra careful. The Market has no-violence restrictions and stuff, so we're safe that way, even from all the things showing up that aren't locals. But just the Market itself is..."

"Really big and confusing, sure."

"Not just that. Yes, you need to stick with me, and especially by Ashling. Since people who are still lost in the Market when it disappears..."

Megan paled a little. "Wait, so 'poof'? No 'we'll let you wait for your ride'?"

Lani shook her head, "Poof, gone. And anyone still inside when they do are lost 'til at least the next time it shows up. Sometimes they're never found at all."

Justin looked up from his menu at that, but seemed to think his feelings on being lost in a temporal anomaly went without saying.

"Okay," Megan said. "So no getting lost. Thankfully, we have a pixie."

"Right. And then buying things..."

"Like I have enough money for even one moving painting. And where would I put it?"

"I'm serious, Megan. They don't really take money anyway. It's like weird barter. Some of the vendors will take almost anything. And they really do sell everything. But the price isn't always obvious."

"So, like, 'trade one or two of my paintings for something' kind of barter?" Megan looked more interested, and not at all prone to caution.

"Maybe, but also, well, like the old stories of bargains with Faeries. Some of them will take stuff like earliest memories, or the color of your eyes. And they really will take them. You need to be super careful what you bargain with."

That got Megan's attention, and a short silence followed while Megan mentally bounced back and forth between taking in Lani's intended caution and trying to figure out not only what someone with the color of their eyes taken would look like, but how one would extract that. Deciding a change of subject was needed, finally, Megan broke the silence. "So, Justin. How've the first few days of GED studying gone?"

"Well enough. Better than school did." Justin and the Kahales had come to the unanimous decision that attempting one semester as a 'foreign exchange student' had been enough of an effort. So of course, as soon as the school year had ended, he'd gotten right to work on what he was told had to happen to replace school.

"All that trying to explain math and science," Megan reflected. "And English turned out to be the worst trouble." Granted, they were lucky he could speak modern English at all, but that had been what the magical crash course was for. "It's funny— not funny ha-ha, funny peculiar—that I've kind of found Shakespeare a bit easier since all the Faerie stuff started happening."

"I apologize again for my poor handling of information."

"Hey, I totally believe you about Henry IV being a jerkface, but no one at school can know you knew the guy personally."

"Hardly personally. I was just familiar with the sort of things he did, politically. It was part of the reason I was sent on my original quest: rallying the populace against people like him. And it turns out he won. He ended up king. Plays were written about heroes fighting *for* his injustices. It's ... uncomfortable."

"So... are you sorry you're not back then, sorting stuff out?"

"I doubt I would have been able to, and I can't be sorry for what was out of my control. I'm proud to wear your favor." Justin touched the Seahawks hat Megan had given him at court the previous fall. He wore it constantly most places, but set it beside them when at the table. "We are here, and it is now ..." He stared at the menu. "We are here, it is now, and cheese is an appetizer."

"They didn't have cheese in the 14th Century?"

"Of course, but you ate it last. Fruit first. Cheese last. Basic health guideline."

"The night we met, I saw you have a hunk of cheese *with* an apple."

"We were working."

"It's only unhealthy if you're not working?"

"The golems were going to be more unhealthy. It's better to have a full stomach as quickly as possible when lives are at stake."

As usual, Megan found it hard to debate Justin's sensibility, and didn't have much time, anyway. Their number was called, and Justin helpfully slid out of the booth to go fetch the tray.

When he had gone for the food, Lani leaned in closer to Megan. "You really ought to ask him out, you know."

Megan blushed. "We've been over this. It's... not a good idea."

"Megan, seriously, just ask him to be your date at the fair, or something. It doesn't have to be a big deal."

"It is a big deal. He's still figuring out a lot of things about this time. And I don't want to take advantage of him or something."

"You've seen the way he looks at you, right? And the way he calls you 'my lady,' when he can get away with it?"

"That's professional, to him, the princess and her knight thing. I don't want him saying yes out of just... uhm, an obligation thing."

"Admirable sentiment, but I think you're wrong. Ask him."

"Why don't you ask him out, if he's so perfect?"

Lani rolled her eyes. "He's like my brother. Okay, so he's nothing like my actual brother—Justin totally doesn't get LEGOs, doesn't get all excited about everything, and still doesn't see why Mack insisted on the name *Space Ship!* for a car. But you know what I mean. We're like the Wonder Twins of practical solutions."

Megan snorted. "Okay, now that's true. Your powers combine, and the problems line up in neat little rows."

Lani grinned. "Sorted by severity and time-crunch. Besides, Megan, aside from the whole school thing, he's doing fine. He works in the garden. He fixed Mom's pottery wheel. He's teamed up with Mack and promised my parents he'd help take care of any puppy Mack might receive... and my parents actually believe him. Seriously, just ask."

Megan shook her head. "I can't. I'm going to have enough trouble just convincing my Mom to let me go to the Fremont Fair with you. No way could I explain asking a boy out. You know how she gets."

As Lani was about to respond, Justin returned with their lunch. Megan shifted the topic, and the half-menehune, the 14th-Century knight, and the Princess of the Unseelie Court talked over food, even managing to touch on subjects of a completely non-magical, non-historic, but non-dating nature. Justin refused to touch the mozzarella sticks until he'd cleared his plate.

Once everyone was done eating, they filed out, Justin getting the door with his usual way of looking around like they might be attacked at any moment. After all they'd been through in the Fall semester, Megan couldn't completely blame him. Then he took the back seat of *Space Ship!* after politely helping Megan into the front. The car, ostensibly a '92 Chevy but a little something special after being a father-daughter project for a menehune family, took off smoother than outsiders might expect, and soon they dropped Megan off back home at the plain, off-white house in West Seattle.

Chapter 3: Green Pills

Megan came home to find her mother staring at a piece of paper: a report card.

"It's in?" Megan said. "Awesome."

Sheila O'Reilly blinked at her arrival. "Maybe we should get you tutoring?" her mother said, staring somehow distantly at the paper.

It was Megan's turn to blink. "Mom, it's Summer. And I already have tutoring. It's called Lani."

"Is everything okay with your medication?"

"Yes. I've been taking it just right." Of course, the right amount of ADHD medication was, admittedly, different than the amount her mother had convinced herself Megan should be taking, which had left Megan's life in a haze until Lani had forced a secret readjustment. Yet another thing in her life her mother didn't know.

Her mother gestured with the report card. "B in Math, B- in Chemistry."

"All right!" Megan had almost been worried for a minute there, by her mother's concerned, blinking reaction. "B in this case stands for 'Bow before me, O synthetic division.'"

"I thought you were doing well."

"I did do well. I finally managed to get synthetic division to work at all. And look, GPA's the best I've ever had." Megan pointed as she stepped beside her mother. This was an accomplishment. This was great. And despite knowing better, Megan couldn't help looking at her mother, waiting for the realization that she could be happy. It never came.

"Yes." Sheila O'Reilly sighed. "If one factors in..." her mother almost had to take a breath to say it. "Music Appreciation and Art."

"Yep. I got my plus back in Art." Having briefly lost it during her overmedicated phase had been embarrassing.

"And if you were just planning on art school, there'd be nothing to worry about."

Art school was, indeed, one of the things Megan was planning. But every time she tried to mention it, there was this strange, brittle look in her mother's eyes, somewhere between confusion, concern, and pain.

"Still, not bad, right?"

"...No," her mother said. "Not bad. I'm sure there's something we can do, though. You know I want to help."

"I know." Megan certainly knew. Aside from professional concerns, helping was the only thing her mother managed any interest in doing. "Work okay?"

"Work is fine."

Megan managed to deflect some more questions regarding her grades, scholarships, and Summer tutors, partly by helping noisily with dinner preparations. She was proud of her report card after the struggles she'd had, and especially with trying to learn magic from Ashling on the side all the while. Her mother stopped fretting enough to get food served and to take out the bottle of green pills to take with the meal. Megan wondered, as she had many times these past months, how well those worked for people whose conditions had nothing to do with being 'fae-touched.' Better, probably.

They ate quietly for a little bit, before Megan's thoughts wandered back to the Fair—and to Cassia's band. The satyress had cheerfully announced that Sax & Violins would be playing her neighborhood's Event of the Season. That took Megan to considering some of the CDs in her mother's box of keepsakes in her closet.

"Hey, Mom, when I was a baby or before I was born..." Megan tried to keep her deeper breath unnoticeable. "...did you ever play the Fremont Solstice Fair?"

And there it was: that bright, brittle look in her mother's eyes at having to wrap her mind around acknowledging the fact of her former music career.

"Yeah," Sheila O'Reilly said quietly. "I did stuff like that then." And the edge of fear in the look got a little stronger. "You said those voice lessons were just so you could join the school choir."

"Yeah, they were," Megan said quickly. "I was just curious, Mom. I promise."

Her mother breathed. "Why were you curious?"

"Was thinking of going to the fair with the Kahales. Just to watch and eat the food and hang with Lani. The whole family's going. Well, except Mr. K. He's out of town again for work." Out of this facet of reality, technically, but as far as Megan's mother knew, Lani's father was human. Of course, as far as Megan's mother knew, Megan's father had been human.

"If Mrs. Kahale takes you, that's reasonable," Sheila O'Reilly agreed as she looked at her watch and picked up the computer bag by her chair to take out her laptop.

"It's 7:30," she said simply, and Megan needed no other explanation. Wednesday evenings at 7:30, her mother took an hour to clear out her spam folder—after carefully checking any work-based e-mails. Plenty of the live music events that Sheila helped administrate, but never attended, had near-last-minute changes or questions, making Wednesdays and Thursdays busy days.

Once the dishes were cleaned, Megan headed back towards her room, but then detoured. Knowing that her mother would be occupied for some time, Megan quietly headed for her mother's room, and the box of keepsakes hidden there. It was precisely as Megan had left it last time, which was exactly how she'd found it originally. As far as she'd been able to tell from the dust on it, it had gone untouched on the high closet shelf for over a decade, along with the old bass. That, much as she longed to, she couldn't touch, for fear her mother might notice it was disturbed, but the box, Megan was pretty sure, was practically forgotten.

She shifted the carefully folded tour T-shirts aside and started going through the CDs. Fourth one down, after looking through the songs, she found what she was looking for—one of the compilation albums included two songs recorded live at the Fremont Solstice Fair.

She was just starting to put things back the way she found them, aside from the borrowed CD, when a voice startled her enough to drop the CDs she was holding.

"Tsk, amateur. Not even wearing gloves."

"Ashling! Shhh!"

"You shhh," said the tiny amber figure on the carpet, torn butterfly wings dangling from her shoulders. "Your mom can't even hear me. I'm like the wind. And possibly some other '80s power ballads."

"Did you walk all the way down the hallway?"

"More discreet than riding," the pixie said.

"Waiting would have been even more discreet."

"You'd be more discreet with me showing you how to sneak stuff."

Megan quickly shuffled the CDs back into place and put the shirts back, then returned the box, trying to get out of the room in case her exclamation drew any attention from the kitchen, while Ashling continued mixing tips on breaking and entering with old song lyrics. Megan did hold on to the single CD, and she headed straight for her room with it after making sure the hall was clear.

Ashling's crow companion, the Count, was waiting patiently for them on the bust of Athena Megan had been given, crafted in Faerie for just this purpose. Lani had helpfully made a shelf for her next to the bedroom door. Her mother had questioned it, but mostly let it go the way she did many minor issues that Megan could reasonably describe as 'an art thing.'

"What are you doing here? Did my dad send you?"

"Yeah. Did you hear about the Market?"

"Yeah," Megan said, fidgeting with the CD. "Lani told me."

"But did she tell you about the animate piggy banks?"

"No. She mentioned moving paintings, though. That might be nice." Megan stopped suddenly as she was putting the CD in the player. "Wait, why would I want an animate piggy bank?"

"Who doesn't like getting bacon for their loose change? And the paintings? Those're nothing. Wait'll you see the lamp exchange."

Megan struggled slightly to regain a grasp of the conversation. "So Dad...?"

"Oh, yeah, he wants to ask you something. In person. So let's go tomorrow, okay?"

"Okay," Megan said as she put the headphones on, listening to the voice that was so much younger, but recognizably her mother's.

'Why is it Monday? / And how am I hungover from your laugh? / Why is it Monday? / And where did we get a balloon giraffe?'

The crowd went wild as her parents rocked out, when no one understood that something was burning away.

Chapter 4: Still New

An Teach Deiridh, The Last Home, lay in bright and golden sunshine, because it had been back under the reign of the Seelie court for nearly two months, but Riocard, the Unseelie King, still strutted across the front lawn like he owned the place to greet his daughter.

Once they actually reached each other, however, both their smiles got a little more strained with brief, awkward hesitation before finally they hugged.

"I *will* get the hang of that eventually," Riocard muttered as they parted.

"S'okay," Megan said. "We're new at this."

"Yeah," Ashling piped up above them. "Hugs. Court. Not enough practice." From atop the Count's back, she shrugged her tattered Painted-Lady wings. "Speaking of practice, not much new to report on her studies, Sir, but they should be getting better now that there isn't school to get in the way."

"Of course. Thank you for your efforts, Ashling, and for bringing her over for this visit." The king also nodded to the crow. "Counts-to-18, you're looking well. There must be something to be said for Seattle's rat problem."

"Caw."

Riocard shifted a foot to look at his brown leather boots, then shook his head, coal-black hair falling behind his shoulders. "Thank you, but these are actually quite old." The king looked back to Megan. "How..." and the awkwardness was apparently not yet over. "How is your mother?" There was nothing worried or brittle in the sidhe king's ice-blue eyes, just genuine curiosity—and perhaps an acknowledgment that a sad thing existed.

"She's Mom."

"Ah. As she's been for some time, as I understand it. Let's get inside. How are *you* feeling about your magical progress?"

"Getting somewhere, I think. The winds and stuff are easiest, still. I keep practicing healing and inspiration, since Ashling says those are things most bards can do, but... uhm, it's hard to tell if I'm getting better or not. I don't really want to injure myself, and Ashling is enthusiastic at random times as it is. And..." Megan paused.

"And?"

"And it was getting easier in big leaps and things back in October and November, then it got a little bit trickier. And then Spring hit, and half of it was like starting over."

Riocard glanced at Ashling. "Seasonal affinity?"

The pixie nodded. "She takes before her old man."

Megan blinked. "Okay, so I sort of get it. Dad's all about Winter: snow, ice, and...uhm, Winter things. But shouldn't that be 'takes after'?"

"I said what I meant," Ashling said.

"What she means," Riocard stepped in, "is that you're an Autumn."

"Caw."

"Yes, Counts-to-Eighteen, she has numerous characteristics marking her as a Spring, and I'm sure she'd love to take you shopping as her fashion consultant for back-to-school. At the moment, however, we're discussing magic, not sweaters. And I believe there's some restriction or other about taking crows into shopping malls."

"Caw."

"Agreed." Then Riocard turned his attention back to Megan. "As my affinity is Winter, it sounds like yours may be Autumn."

"I am pretty good with the dancing leaves," Megan said.

"Trust me, just the beginning. I'm sure Ashling will be happy to continue helping you, and we'll consider that a focus area for now."

Ashling nodded enthusiastically. "I'm good at focus."

Megan thought about responding, then gave up and looked back to her father. "How about you? With a little extra time on your hands, have you been looking over that list of people you were talking about?"

"No. I've never been the sort of man who was good at looking over lists. The rigors of choosing a new seneschal are exactly the sort of thing I used to have a seneschal for." He frowned, and for a moment the only sounds were their footsteps on the smooth stone of the front halls of An Teach Deiridh and the flap of the Count's wings.

Then, Megan sniffed. "Oh my gosh, that smells delicious. Can I get some of those cinnamon rolls, Dad?"

"Certainly," he said. "Stop right into the kitchen and ask. I'll wait in my room."

Megan raised an eyebrow. "You'll wait?"

"I invite many kinds of trouble, dearest," the king said. "The result of looming over brownies in their own kitchens does not happen to be among them."

"Okay." Megan headed into the indicated kitchen—and almost smack into a small tow-headed figure in baggy clothes. "Oh! Hi, Kerr!"

The brownie looked flustered. "Hi, Highness." And there was that sort-of-bow, sort-of-curtsey again. Megan had known the brownie for nearly eight months now, and she was still slightly confused.

"So, uhm, I wanted to tell you that the cinnamon rolls smell delicious, and I was wondering if any were available."

"Oh. Thank you. Yes, you can have one, of course." Kerr scurried over to cut one from the cooling pan. "Is Lani with you?" Kerr asked.

"Thanks. No, she's back in Seattle with Mack." Seeing that the ruddy little face looked slightly less cheerful at that, Megan added. "I'll tell her..." But talking about Kerr always felt complicated when Megan didn't even... "Look, Kerr, I'm sorry to ask abruptly, but are you a boy or a girl?"

Kerr shuffled slightly while handing Megan a small plate with the cinnamon roll on it. "Not really," Kerr said.

"Oh." Oh. Megan smiled. "Okay, thanks. I'll tell Lani you said hi. Hope we see you at the market sometime."

Kerr smiled, then gave another little bow-curtsey. "That would be great."

Ashling returned from whatever food had attracted the Count's attention, and they made their way into the 'Unseelie wing' of the castle. Megan had grown somewhat accustomed to everything from the thornvines to the sometimes macabre artwork. None of it spoiled her appetite.

When they reached the entwined-wood meeting table in the western tower, her father was waiting, as were two leopards curled up around the roots beneath it. Cassia, horned and hooved and bedecked in bronze that nearly matched her skin, leaned against a wall, apparently watching her cats lounge until Riocard got back.

"Hey, Megan. Ashling. Count," the satyress said.

"Hey, Cassia. Maxwell. Jude," Megan replied, crouching to scritch the latter just under the edge of his aviator helmet—while holding her plate high over her head with the other hand. "You're actually in Faerie for a change."

Cassia grinned. "Your dad made it worth my while to hang out. We managed to have a good time in Faerie without even stabbing anything. You didn't bring Lani or Sir Blushes-a-lot?"

"They're babysitting." Megan sat down next to her father and started properly on her cinnamon roll. "And probably making contingency plans for tomorrow while they're at it."

"Makes sense. I'm definitely looking forward to playing both fairs. Maybe I'll do some shopping while I'm at it."

"That reminds me, Megan," her father said. "I should get you one of my bookmarks, let you do a little easy shopping."

"You realize how weird that sounds, right?" Megan asked.

His eyebrow raised. "Well, someone's been taking her medication." But he smiled as he grabbed a heavy leather-bound volume on the end of the table, opened it, and removed an old baseball card.

Megan managed to keep herself from reaching with sticky fingers. "So, you're saying that they'll take baseball cards as payment at this Goblin Market?"

Riocard shook his head and smiled. "No. I'm saying they'll take that baseball card as payment at the Goblin Market. You ought to be able to get just about anything you want for it."

"Uhm, I'm not sure I want to know, but exactly why is this one so special?"

Riocard chuckled. "The easy answer is this: it's one of my bookmarks. I'll want it back."

"How are they supposed to know that?" Megan asked as she licked a little bit of icing off her fingers.

"Trust me, they'll know. The merchants at the Market have a way of knowing the value of things."

"Okay," Megan said. "I'll trust you on that. So, what did you want to ask me?"

"As Cassia said, she'll be playing both festivals. I'll only have time for one concert, on the Honored Guests' dais. I was hoping you'd join me."

"Sure. Why wouldn't—oh. Is the Queen going to be one of the other Honored Guests? And her... guy?"

"We'll be joining Orlaith, yes," Riocard said. "Her General Inwar hopes to make it as well, though he may be detained by his other responsibilities."

"Isn't he her bodyguard or something?"

"He's certainly something, but he's served the role of bodyguard among his other security functions, yes. He has ever since he affiliated with An Teach Deiridh."

"Affiliated? What, like the menehune? So he really isn't sidhe? Is that why he's so ...chilly?"

"As Ljosalfar go, Inwar has generally struck me as quite warm and compromising."

"Leos-alf-har?" Megan attempted.

"Light-elves." For once, Ashling's linguistic interjection was helpful.

"But indeed," Riocard continued, "General Inwar is from Scandinavia. And, to wind about the digression, he may or may not be at the concert in the Goblin Market, but his Queen certainly will. So, Megan, will you join us on the dais?"

Megan sighed. "Well, okay. No hard feelings, after all." That got a very approving smile from her father. Megan had picked up pretty quickly that he wasn't going to let a little thing like being set up to be betrayed and imprisoned, almost leading to a seasonal magical disaster, spoil a perfectly cordial professional relationship with the Seelie Queen.

"Okay," Megan repeated. "Wouldn't miss it."

Chapter 5: Backstage

Mrs. Kahale was saying something, but Megan was watching for the sign. *"Welcome to Fremont, Center of the Universe,"* it said. Despite not being that long a drive, coming to the quirky artists' neighborhood had always felt like entering a whole different world. At least until Megan had actually entered a whole different world that made this place look sane. A few blocks later was the statue of Lenin. She supposed some things about Fremont might always look odd, even after having seen Faerie.

"Megan, Honey..." Mrs. K's voice cut through the reverie. "Could you make Mack a maze for his LEGOs?" It was a familiar request. Megan pulled the pad and pen stashed on the back of the seat and set to work, designing a maze with an outer border in the shape of a hard hat as she listened to Mrs. Kahale's reminders.

"All right, girls—and Justin—we'll drop you off, Mack and I will run errands while you go to Cassia's band gathering and the Other Thing, and then we'll pick you up at the barrier on Phinney at 4:30."

"At the barrier on Phinney at 4:30," Megan repeated in near-unison with Lani as, within the maze, she carefully added some LEGO hazards, like a LEGO-ized minotaur, in the dead ends.

Mrs. Kahale continued. "Now Lani's got her backpack, but I know you'll probably want to eat at the Other Thing. Please make sure you get something sort of resembling actual meals, not all sugar."

"Don't worry, Mrs. K," Megan said as she handed the new maze to an appreciative Mack. "If Lani doesn't have a food pyramid on hand, Justin probably has a cheese schedule." Megan grinned when Lani smirked at her.

Megan's mother might object if she knew Lani's mother wouldn't be keeping a direct eye on them the whole time—even without knowing anything else—but they'd have her number, and she'd be close—in terms of the real world, anyway.

"All of you, stay out of trouble, be very careful, and don't hesitate to call if there's any problems, okay?"

The three agreed, thanking her for the ride, before piling out of the car. Justin was carrying a bass guitar case. Megan hadn't yet asked why.

Cassia met them at the barrier, along with three other girls. Megan had looked up Cassia's band, Sax & Violins, but due to her mother's restrictions, their shows this weekend would be her first chance to see the band live.

"All right, people," Cassia said. "Our show isn't until tomorrow, but we're helping out some friends. You of course know Violet Baptiste, the world's hottest fiddler." Cassia's bronze-toned hand clasped the slightly darker hand of the girl next to her, whose dreadlocked hair sported streaks of, predictably, violet. Megan had met Cassia's girlfriend in passing and nodded politely before Cassia's introductory attention moved to the other two.

"This is Nell, our lead singer," she said, gesturing to the tiny, delicate, girl with long, chestnut hair. As Megan looked at her, the girl's visage shifted slightly, which Megan had started getting used to, when meeting faeries and other inhuman folk. It was mostly subtle, but small details drew her eye, like the slightly webbed fingers, and the fact that Nell seemed to have a second set of eyelids—nearly clear membranes that closed side-to-side instead of up-and-down—under her regular eyelids. Megan wasn't sure what it meant, but apparently Cassia wasn't the only non-human in the band.

"And Erin, our bassist," Cassia added, pointing to a strawberry blonde with short curls, wearing horn-rimmed glasses, a Dresden Dolls promotional t-shirt, and cargo pants.

"So you're Megan O'Reilly," Erin said, extending a hand to Megan first. "I saw Late to the Party play on their last tour. One of my first concerts, and part of the reason I started playing bass. Your mother's work was... well, incendiary."

"So I've heard." Megan said.

The band members said their hellos to Lani and Justin as well, then the lot of them followed Cassia towards the main stage.

The rest of the band was hard at work around the stage when they got there. Katja, the band's second violinist, was talking with some people on stage, probably one of the other bands. The cowgirl hat Megan had seen on the tall blonde in all the band photos was there, but for set-up time, she'd apparently exchanged the bikini top and denim skirt for a t-shirt and jeans.

The last member of the band, who usually went by Cris on the album covers and their website, was off to one side of the stage, helping the roadies haul boxes. The short-haired drummer's arms were works of art, bright tattoo sleeves all accented by musical bars that wound around her arms with notes and what Megan suspected were lyrics mixed in. Given the completeness of the work, and hints of ink on the woman's neck, just showing over the collar of her black tank top, Megan suspected there was a whole lot more artwork covered up.

Cassia went through the rest of the introductions, showing the girls around the backstage area, and introducing them to a few of the other local musicians. When she got called over to offer her advice on a set list, Megan took the opportunity to talk to Erin a little more. "So, how did you meet Cassia, anyway?"

"Through Violet. We went to school together here. We played a few gigs in the area before she met Cassia, and S & V started."

"So, you're going to be playing both shows?" Since Megan hadn't gotten any particularly magical or Faerie-like vibes off of Erin, she was trying to figure out exactly how the system worked. There were plenty of stories of humans pulled into Faerie, but she hadn't seen any normal people, aside from Justin— to whatever degree a boy from centuries in the past was normal—when she was there.

"Yeah, the band sort of knows what's up, but only the very basics, and we don't ask questions."

"Why is that?"

"Because that's one of the first things Nell told us, and Cassia kind of agreed. You'll find plenty of people in Fremont who believe in some very out-there things. The idea that Faerielands and whatever exist wasn't the biggest of shocks, but I believe them when they say we really don't want to know, or get more involved. We'll go; we'll watch the pretty lights; we'll eat what Nell says is okay, and we'll play. The rest of the time, this city is enough weirdness for me."

Megan nodded. "Center of the Universe and all."

Erin grinned. "Center of the Universe."

"So what's Nell's story?"

"You'd be better off asking her. All I know is she and Cassia have the same 'Old Country,' and Nell likes to stay the heck away from anything to do with the place or any place like it. She lives a few doors down from me and doesn't go out much except to perform. Whatever she is, she has an incredible voice. I'm surprised we haven't met. You've known Cassia for a while, right?"

"Since October," Megan said. "Lani introduced us. But my mom doesn't really like me going to concerts or things like that."

"Wait, Sheila O'Reilly? Seriously? Why?"

Megan paused. The girl said they tried to avoid knowing too much. "It's complicated. She just doesn't want me getting into trouble, I guess."

"Oh... okay." Erin looked slightly forlorn. "When I heard you were going to be here, I was kind of hoping I might get a chance to meet her, too."

"She doesn't really do shows. Sorry."

They were going to talk more, but Cassia was calling, holding something in hand and waving. She stood next to one of the roadies, who had to be one of the biggest men Megan had ever seen—and the eyepatch he wore didn't do anything to make him look friendlier. Megan headed for the pair. Or possibly quartet— Megan noted that right beside Cassia was a basket containing two spotted kittens, one in an aviator helmet.

"The boys are coming?" Megan asked.

"Jude doesn't trust me to shop for his Pulp Flying Ace Adventure Hour records by myself." Cassia handed her a tan-and-green laminated slip of paper, bearing the words BACKSTAGE PASS. "These will get you through the gate, and over to the market. Finn here will be keeping an eye on the passage a little." As Megan got used to the big man's presence, and started to associate him with Faerie things like knowing where the gate was, the massive figure began to resemble the other trolls Megan had seen in Faerie.

"Finn?" Megan asked, extending a hand. "So, you're the bouncer?"

The troll grinned, displaying questionable dentistry and some jagged teeth. "Nah, just filling in. Mostly a roadie for Cass and Nell. And a model." He shifted the meat-laden sticks held in his hand to the other to free a hand, wiped it on his jeans, and shook her hand carefully.

"A model?" Megan blinked, looking confused.

Cassia filled in. "Finn is very proud of having helped to inspire the sculpture under the Aurora Bridge."

"Ah. That makes ...sense." Megan looked at Finn. "So you're an under-the-bridge-type troll?"

"Once upon a time," Finn said, smiling wryly. "Nowadays, I've got a great apartment. The upstairs neighbors are just as noisy, but I like the place." He then glanced at his snack, shifting one of the sticks back and offering it to Megan. "Goat kebab?"

"Uhm, no thanks," she replied. "We'll get something at the Market."

The troll nodded, gesturing for the girls, the kittens, and Justin to follow. Eventually, he led them to a door that should have led to a recessed area under the stage, hidden away amidst the sound equipment, crates, and instrument cases—to which Justin quietly added his. Megan wanted to remember to ask about that.

"Right through here," Finn explained, opening the door. Inside, at first, there was only darkness. When she started to see the reflected glint, within the passage, of the bluish glow of balefire, Megan knew better than to look. She closed her eyes and walked through the doorway.

Chapter 6: The Goblin Market

The underside of the stage smelled like dirt, grease, stale beer, smoke breaks, and smoke breaks that weren't entirely tobacco. Over the fading sounds of instruments tuning, Megan could hear the crackling of the balefires, but there was no heat.

The smells and sounds of Fremont disappeared as she took another step forward. They were replaced by cackling laughter on one side, which was then overwhelmed by the sound of sobbing. She nearly opened her eyes, but remembered Justin's ordeal—his lost mentor, the lost centuries, all from wide-eyed misdirection on the paths. Megan kept her eyes shut tightly and kept walking.

A few moments followed where she couldn't tell if she was falling, being spun around, or both. When that settled, she was hit by conflicting sounds: folk music, stomping feet, and laughter from her left, and from the distant right, discordant heavy metal and what sounded like chainsaws on steel. Her nose picked up freshly turned earth, livestock, fires, unwashed bodies, washed bodies with all sorts of scented things, and less identifiable impressions all hitting her at once.

The real impact came when she finally did open her eyes and was assaulted by the sight of the Market, a mile or more of sheer spectacle of colors and motion: signs, tents, jugglers, acrobats, pegasus rides, and countless other attractions and distractions.

"About darn time," Ashling said. "I've been right here waiting forever."

"Caw."

"I know time is relative here, Count. That just makes it worse."

"Caw."

"Yes, it does. Now let's get going. I only get to shop for hyacinth-petal edible fashions once a year."

Lani nodded. "Okay, Cassia, do Jude and Maxwell still want to spend a while in the giant non-orientable cat tree?"

"Yep. Come on boys."

Megan looked at Lani. "Non-orientable cat tree?"

"You know cat trees, right? Those whole carpeted scratching-posty-structures?"

"Yes. That's not the question."

"Okay, you know Moebius strips, right?" Lani's finger sketched a twisted circle in the air. "They only have one side?"

"...Yes."

"Well imagine a whole bunch of big ones made of carpet and all glued together at the ends."

Megan decided to stick with "I'm glad the cats will have somewhere to play." She continued walking as the colors and sounds and smells filled the air.

Megan stopped and stared, wide-eyed. 'Souls Sold,' read a messily scrawled sign in one corner.

"It's okay, Megan," Lani said. "It really is. That's a shoemaker. He's just really bad at spelling."

Writing also did not seem to be the forte of the hag stirring a giant brass kettle. The sign saying 'SoUp' appeared to be have been etched with rusty red pen. Megan was going to choose to believe that the hag simply had rusty red pens lying around.

She also was relieved to see a nice, normal hot dog stand to the left. As Megan reached into her pocket for the baseball card, Lani put a hand on her arm. "Don't," the shorter girl said.

Justin looked at the stand, just a touch green. "I don't trust the hot dogs in your world, much less these."

"Hold out, and we'll split some roast chicken," Lani suggested. "Or the curries in the central bazaar: they're guaranteed real mutton from sheep that were always sheep."

Megan nodded, supposing that some of those thoughts were certainly enough to take the edge off her appetite. Still, she looked over quickly when she heard cries about eggs and was surprised by the museum-like display cases.

"Fabergé eggs! Golden goose-eggs! Stone eggs of the Ephesian Lady!" announced the fancily-dressed creature.

"The Ephesian Temple was one of the old Seven Wonders of the World, right?" Megan remarked to her friends. Art History really was the best history.

"Well, not every temple they built in that spot over the centuries," Cassia said with a shrug. "Just the one that was destroyed by H—"

"Don't you dare," Lani interrupted her. "Don't you dare say it. Don't give him the satisfaction unless you can name the architects and every member of the work crew."

"Hey, even I'm not old enough to have known any of those people, and nobody took down the names of work crews."

"Well, they *made something*. All he did was break it. And he thought that made him special, and I won't hear you make him right. He gets to be nobody. That's what he gets."

Megan wanted to give Lani's righteous civil-engineering indignation the moment it deserved, but she'd just noticed something. "Oooh."

It was the way the vibrations rippled through the paint that did it. Or maybe it was the colors. Megan walked closer and closer to the painting, stepping past a jade statue. The painting was very much like something she'd do, but unlike any of her works, the painting was alive. The Autumn scene was full of red and orange leaves blanketing the ground and trees lining the sides of a stream with not-yet-fallen leaves in the same shades. A soft wind carried the leaves around in small eddies and shook the branches gently.

Every now and then, a bigger gust blew, sweeping up more leaves and disturbing the hiding butterflies, which drifted higher, eventually flying out of the panel, or re-settling as the wind did. Despite watching, transfixed, for several minutes, Megan couldn't see any repetition or pattern.

"Interested?" asked the jade-colored woman.

Megan nearly jumped as what she had presumed to be a statue spoke. Then she nodded. "How much? I mean...how's this?" She pulled the baseball card out of her pocket and handed it over.

The woman looked at the card. "Certainly. And would Your Highness like this delivered to your room at An Teach Deiridh?"

"Um, sure." She couldn't take it to her house, after all. It actually took a few moments to reflect on the fact that the woman must have meant her father's room, as Megan didn't recall having a room at An Teach Deiridh. But there was no time to clarify, because as the painting was being taken from the market by a pair of trolls, Megan's eye was drawn by another shop being set up in an empty space a few lots down.

In truth, shop might be giving it too much credit. A goblin with an especially long, hooked nose rolled a rock that was larger than he was into the spot. Megan drifted closer while the goblin somehow tacked a poster, which included some writing and a picture of himself, up to the front of the rock. The next few minutes saw him dragging boxes and crates up next to the rock, and then unpacking all manner of collapsible shelves from them and lining the shelves with vials. Looking at his supplies, there was no way all of it should have fit in the relatively few containers.

She finally got close enough to read the poster. Unlike a lot of the scratches and uneven letters, this was neat, even stylized.

THE MEDICINE SHOW
Ills cured, ailments resolved, curses lifted, snakes oiled.
Satisfaction guaranteed.

"Walk right over. Step right up. Ladies, Gentlemen, and Others, my practice does not deal in generified panaceas. All treatments are specialized to the condition, whether one needs the cure for the Black Death, a black eye, a black mood, something you painted black but now want your window back—but do keep in mind, ladies and gentlemen, that 'not being romantically interested in the person others might prefer them to be' is not, in fact, an ailment. Unlike some two-bit operations, I do not insult my customers' intelligence with love potions."

How many times, Megan wondered, had the guy had to tell someone that, to end up putting it in his sales patter? She was glad that at least, whatever Lani might randomly advise, there was no way there'd ever be any magical pressure about dating Justin—or anyone. And Lani was wrong about Justin, of course.

Lani tapped her on the shoulder.

Megan jumped. "What?"

"You wandered off going 'Ooooh.'"

"Sorry. Bought a painting, and then there was … that guy."

"Yeah," Lani said. "It's interesting and all. But let's go get food, okay?"

"Sure. Where's Ashling?" Megan looked at the bazaar-like area up ahead and wondered if there was the lamp exchange the pixie had mentioned.

The group started towards the bigger tents, with the promised curry. "She was with us for a little bit. Then she said she needed to check something out. I'm sure she'll be right..."

There was a loud squawking ahead, accompanied by a shout. Megan had by this point learned just enough Gaelic to wonder if Ashling even knew the target's mother.

Chapter 7: Collector

Megan's question was answered immediately as she managed to parse the next string of shrill words floating over the market, which called into question whether the target ever had a mother. When the screaming and cawing didn't stop, Megan took off alongside Lani, just behind Cassia and Justin, already running in the direction of the pixie's voice.

"That last part sounded different," Megan called to Lani as they darted towards the outbursts.

"That's because she switched to German."

"Well, it does make better heavy metal for a reason," Megan conceded breathlessly before another, even harsher string of sounds followed. When Lani winced, Megan asked, "What?"

"That was really vicious in Klingon."

"Of course you speak Klingon."

They emerged from a row of vendors in time to see a tall, auburn-haired man shoving people out of his way as he ran. Ashling, astride the Count, was in hot pursuit from above. That was all the inspiration it took for Cassia to join in, racing after the man, knocking over a couple of people just as they were getting up. After sharing a glance, and trying to be more cautious of those around, the three teens took off after them.

The man knocked over a pot of SoUp—and its vendor with it. Some of the ingredients scrambled away on varying numbers of limbs. Recovering his balance, he evaded a dive from the crow-mounted pixie and took off running again.

When the Count next dove—and the man appeared ready to avoid the bird—Ashling leapt off the crow in flight, managing to catch on to one of the pouches at his belt. Noticing the added weight and movement, the man alternately tried grabbing for her, or shoving her away.

Ashling kept darting about and finding handholds, evading his grip. He finally caught hold of the pixie by one leg, pulling her away. Something came away from his pouch in her hands as he tried to hold on.

Cassia's war cry carrying over the crowd alerted him, and instead of holding on or wrestling for whatever it was, he flung the pixie away towards the satyress. Catching Ashling took only a moment, but it was long enough for him to reach, and duck down another row, out of Megan's sight.

Megan and Lani tried to dodge their away around the crowd enough to reach the others. They caught up with Justin first, then, a short time later, with Cassia, Ashling, and the Count trying to make their way through a dense crowd. They finally regrouped.

"I had him! I had him!" the pixie shouted. "We need to keep looking!"

"Ashling, he's gone. We're not going to find him in that crowd, with all those tents, but we'll keep an eye out. Who is that?"

"The *Butterfly Collector*," Ashling snarled.

"You're sure?" Lani asked, horrified, and staring down the row like she might pick him out of the crowd somehow. Megan, in contrast, was trying not to stare at Ashling's sliced wings.

"I'm going to remember that face. And those hands holding cold iron. And that voice—the poxy bastard went on and on 'til the Count got to me. It's him." Ashling was shaking as she tried to hoist herself back on the Count's back.

"Wow," Megan said, still trying not to look right at the wings. "You don't think he brought cold iron here, do you?"

"He'd have to *really* be a moron," said Cassia. "This crowd would tear him to pieces. Orlaith exiled her own nephew for trying to duel with cold iron once. A mortal, at the Goblin Market..." Cassia trailed off, shaking her horned head, but the implications were clear.

"If this guy really is who Ashling says he is—" Lani began.

"He is," Ashling interjected, scowling.

"Caw."

"You see? The Count never forgets a face—"

"Caw."

"—or a terribly pretentious lapel pin. Seriously, a bronze and ivory bull? That is downright bull—"

"Caw."

"Yeah."

Lani had stood there, mouth still open, waiting to no longer be interrupted. "—then maybe we should see if there's any way to find him."

"And tear his wings off," Ashling added.

"Pretty sure he doesn't have wings," Justin said.

Ashling's scowl just grew more intense. "Arms or legs will do fine, then. Though, really, why stop at 'or'? Let's go with 'and' instead."

"Caw."

"You said it, Count." Ashling's face was getting rather disturbingly gleeful.

Megan raised an eyebrow. "The Count isn't normally real thirsty for non-carrion blood."

"You don't normally see him given cause," Ashling said. "Nobody holds grudges like a crow. Nobody."

A nod of a beak seemed to affirm this.

Megan blinked. "I guess I'll take your word."

Lani interrupted, "So, yeah. Ashling's clearly got a vested interest in looking into the matter."

Cassia handed Ashling what seemed to be a tiny pink headgear constructed out of part of a flower. Ashling accepted it, raised it to her mouth, and took a bite. She sighed loudly. "Not even eating a hat is going to calm me down." But she had another bite anyway.

"She pulled this off of him," Cassia said, holding up a large scrap of paper. "Had to keep her from wrapping herself up." The paper was definitely bigger than Ashling. Lani looked at it, then showed Megan.

It appeared to be a piece of a map. There were four small brownish-red Xs—Megan again chose to assume rusty red ink was involved—impeccably printed at scattered points across the scrap of parchment. One corner of it contained part of a body of water. Beside it was a tiny footnote in Latin. Megan pointed. "What's that say?"

"'Lake shore varies depending on drainage cycle,'" Cassia said.

Megan indicated another footnote. "And this one?"

"'Swamp. Watch for wisps.'"

"Where's all this supposed to be?" Megan asked. "And what's on the other half of the map?" It certainly seemed like the place to start when looking for the owner of the map.

Lani and Cassia looked at the map over her shoulder, then glanced at one another. Then they fidgeted. "Give us a minute," Lani finally said.

"While you take that minute," Justin said. "I'll go pick up the cats from their... tree. I also need to get something from under the stage. I'd hoped to be pleasantly surprised and not need it, but sometimes life is just not surprising."

Chapter 8: Glitter

Lani and Cassia were still huddled over the map, trying to decipher it. Ashling and the Count were pacing back and forth, even if the Count had to make awkward sequential hops to do so. Ashling had quickly finished the treat with which Cassia'd tried to distract her and was now determined to stay ready for ad-hoc limb amputation. Megan was pacing too. She had longer legs than they — and less of Cassia reaching over to put a hand in her way when she got too excited.

Megan's pacing took her further and further each time, and as she did, her thoughts started wandering as well. She started with the map, but didn't even know where it led. The guy Ashling had been chasing was next — the pixie had said something about a fancy lapel pin. Maybe that meant something? She would have sworn she'd seen some kind of motif like that in some of the art when she'd bought her painting. She glanced in the direction of the art dealers, and found herself staring at the hook-nosed goblin on the big rock. What he'd said about curing black moods had stuck with her. Could this be something better than the green pills with supper every night that never seemed to do enough?

"Need a cure, young lady?" asked the goblin standing on top of the boulder.

Megan startled, and glanced up. "Uhm, maybe. You can really cure anything?"

"If you can pay for the cure, certainly."

"What if it's, uhm, not for me?" Megan asked.

"That's fine," the goblin said, gesturing to the rows of vials. "What's the ailment?"

Megan hesitated, entirely unsure about this deal or the goblin. But it was a better chance than she was ever going to get elsewhere. "It's my mom. She kind of spent too much time around a sidhe. I want to sort of...reignite whatever burned out, you know?"

The goblin crouched and leaned in close to her. "How long ago was this?"

"Uhm, about fifteen years. Is that a problem?"

"Problems are just opportunities in work clothes. It's a lot of time to adjust for, but I can fix it... it will just have a suitable mark up in cost. You're sure that's what you want?"

Megan wasn't sure, but she remembered the time she spent overmedicated, living in a fog. She thought about her mother's anti-depressants, her obsessions, and her spending the last decade and a half working event management in the music industry without ever going to shows. She thought about the comments about incendiary bass work—while the bass gathered years of dust alongside the CDs. "I'm sure."

She reached for the baseball card. Her father had said it could pay for nearly anything. Then she remembered the impulse buy. "How much?" she asked, reaching for her wallet instead.

The goblin considered her. "F Sharp," he responded.

Megan blinked, looking at him confused. "What?"

"You have a lovely voice, and it's my favorite note. I'll take F Sharp," he responded, rummaging through his supplies.

Megan took a deep breath, trying to think how that would even work. Then the inspiration took over. "Deal!" she insisted.

The goblin ignored her outstretched hand as he pulled out an odd little tuning fork. "Can I get that in an F Sharp please?"

Megan decided it was a good thing she had perfect pitch. "...~Deal~...?" she sang.

The tuning fork vibrated, and the goblin placed it in a ceramic bowl. He then picked up a ceramic pestle and proceeded, though Megan had no idea how, to crush the tuning fork into a shining silver powder, like glitter. He poured half into a vial that went on his shelf. He then poured the other half into an envelope

He proceeded to get out a pen and write her mother's office address, which Megan had not given him, on the envelope.

"All right," he said. "She'll be the herself she was supposed to be."

Megan was about to ask about side effects, or about how long it would take, or about basic laws of physics or questions of privacy, when Lani's voice drew Megan's attention away from the goblin. "Megan, what did you do?" she asked, running towards

Megan. Cassia wasn't far behind her, with Justin trailing—lugging the instrument case he'd left under the stage.

"It's okay. I have a cure for Mom. That's all."

Lani looked dubiously at the goblin. "You sure you know what you're doing?"

Cassia slapped Lani on the back, almost knocking her over. "Don't worry. The Doctor is good people. If he says he's got a cure, he does. Speaking of which, Doc, Maxwell wants his stuff. Usual payment."

The hook-nosed goblin set to work.

"What stuff?" Megan asked.

"Enchanted catnip. The normal stuff is okay, but whenever the market opens up, I try and get him the good stuff."

"And only Maxwell gets some?"

"Jude's too straight-edge."

Lani sighed. "If Cassia vouches for him, that's... something. I'm not sure exactly what. Just be seriously careful, okay, Megan? We should talk about this. Soon. But not now. We need to hurry while the cats are still keeping Ashling and the Count from leaving without us. We figured out the map. Maybe it's nothing, but I still want to check it out."

Megan sighed. "Check what out?"

"Mag Tuired. If he had a map for it, he might be there."

"He might be, but that's not necessarily a good thing," Justin said, "He obviously knows how to get into Faerie. We surprised him here, but out in the wild..."

Megan nodded. "We'll have to stick together. We'll have you, the cats, and Cassia. And the Count will be watching for trouble."

"We need to help Ashling, and it's not like we can convince her to wait any longer than necessary." Lani added. "Besides, we need to find out what kind of buried treasure—or something—a guy like that would be looking for in Mag Tuired, of all places."

"Sure. There's just one problem," Megan said.

"Oh? And what's that?" Lani asked.

"What the heck is Mo-ay Tu-ra?"

Chapter 9: Mag Tuired

The walk along the lake shore was slow going. It was just as well Cassia hadn't brought her chariot, since as soon as they emerged into the real world, the leopards had ended up looking like kittens again. Megan still wasn't sure how the magic worked. Most of the faeries just ended up looking different, with Ashling looking like a butterfly, and Cassia looking like, well, mostly herself, but lacking horns, a tail, and goat legs. The cats, though, actually seemed to really revert whenever they were somewhere a human might see them.

Indeed, they'd had to accommodate the kittens when they hit the wet, squelching ground. Maxwell had scrambled up Cassia, to rest on her shoulder. Jude, meanwhile, had sat politely, mewing up at Megan until she picked up the kitten in his tiny aviator helmet and placed him to peek out of the pocket of her cargo pants as they walked.

"So, I'm seeing lakes," Megan said. "Weird hills with some kind of stone-agey things on them...some sheep in the distance. Are you sure we didn't come out in the wrong century?"

As it was, Justin was walking around, even if only distant sheep were looking, with the Sword of Light sheathed at his hip, having finally set the instrument case aside just as they left the Market. Megan watched him walk in his particular hypervigilant way for a moment before she managed to look back at Lani questioningly.

Lani sighed. "Past the sheep is a 21st-Century wind farm, Megan. We're not in the Dark Ages; we're in the countryside."

"Okay, so here we are. Middle-of-Nowhere, Ireland. And you promise we'll still get home on time?"

"Yes. We'll be back in Seattle when we left Seattle. That's how the Market works."

"And why is it afternoon in Ireland instead of the middle of the night?"

"Look, don't look a gift temporal-anomaly in the mouth. Think of it like a pause button."

"Is that what it's like?"

"No, but the closest scientific analog is string theory, so we're going to stick with pause buttons, to keep everyone less uncomfortable."

"I can promise you, Lani," Justin said calmly. "That when it comes to the confusions of time, absolutely nothing is going to make me comfortable, so on my account, at least, you needn't worry."

Megan worried for him a little, but she still couldn't get over the place. "Why did the Market even have a path to a bunch of sheep farms? You said it's a historic site?"

"Yeah. Second Battle of Mag Tuired. Now let me make sure we're on the correct side of the lake."

"What did that note mean about the shore changing based on water drainage?"

"Sinkhole," said Cassia grinning. "Considering how it was made, the lake's not exactly going to be stable."

"Do I want to know?" Megan asked. "Okay, yes, I want to know, but *after* you tell me, I might not want to know anymore."

"Of course you want to know," Cassia said, "This is where Balor Birugderc died. It's hard to get a much more epic story."

"What's a Balor?"

"Not what, who. One of the great Fomoire generals. You remember their handiwork in Findias, right? The biggest enemies of the gods... and all the folk whose remnants ended up in An Teach Deiridh."

"Okay, so he died here?"

"Lugh put his spear through his eye. Wish I'd been there to see that. Your dad was there, though. You should ask him about it." Cassia said.

Lani gestured towards the lake. "The legend goes that this is where he fell, and as he died, his eye created the lake here."

"Seriously?"

Lani nodded. "That was his big thing, the evil eye. If he didn't have it covered, it'd burn everything he looked at. And, obviously, if the lake thing is true, he was huge."

Megan glanced out at the water. "That's putting it mildly."

"The Fomoire were bad news. They weren't all that big, but there's a reason the gods left the world in order to keep them from coming back." Lani said.

Megan paused, continuing to study the water, trying to imagine the giant that could have caused it, not liking any of the images in her mind. Finally, "Okay, that is officially the weirdest lake ever."

"Not quite," Lani responded.

"Wait, seriously?" Megan asked, looking dubious.

Cassia glanced at Lani and grinned. "Yeah, I'd say the 'fishing hole' wins."

"Those have to be some seriously messed up fish." Megan said.

"You know more about it than I do," Lani offered, gesturing to Cassia.

"Sure. Messed-up fish, trapped Fomoire, fun stuff. When the gods left, they sealed the Fomoire up. They used all of the enchantments on the city of Gorias to do it, too."

"Gorias," Megan echoed. "That's one of the four lost cities you guys abandoned?"

"I wasn't around yet," Cassia said. "But the Celtic fae, yeah."

Megan glanced at Ashling, just waiting for some contradiction or odd statement about the lake, or fish, or one-eyed giants. The pixie just sat on the Count's back, where he perched on Lani's shoulder, both of them looking more intent than she'd ever seen them. She wasn't even sure how she could tell what the crow was feeling, but it was clear.

"Anyway—" Cassia continued, "They didn't have much choice. All of the magic of the city was channeled to the lake, to freeze it over as a prison. All of the Fomoire who survived the war are down there, under the ice."

That pulled Megan's attention back rapidly. "And they're just, you know, left there unguarded?"

"Hardly. That's Inwar's big job. After what Balor did to his arm, he definitely feels strongly about the Fomoire: left his people completely to affiliate with the Seelie full time, so he could stand watch. He did it on his own for a while, but eventually, more and more people from An Teach Deiridh would come fill in for him, so he could go see Orlaith and help coordinate things. His folk may be cold, but they know war."

"I kind of got that impression," Megan said, "So that's what happened to his arm?"

"And how Orlaith got her scars," Cassia said, nodding. "Just a glance. Inwar shielded her, but she still got burned, and he lost his shield arm."

Megan shuddered: the story with the lake and the giant becoming a lot more real, with a visual reference to what the eye could do. "So, it's like cold iron or something?"

Cassia shook her head. "Burning acid, but it works the same. He could kill faeries or even gods with it. And the wounds never fully heal, no matter how much magic they put into it."

At Ashling's urging, they started walking again, moving along the shore. Megan finally broke the silence again. "So, what happens if the ones in this somehow-weirder lake ever get out? I mean, much as my dad might like it, it's not winter year-round, right?"

"He invests a lot of magic in making sure that doesn't happen. So do the 'fishing trippers,'" Lani explained, "Keeping the lake sealed is the one thing the Seelie and Unseelie can completely agree on. Inwar has soldiers from both sides helping him, and the area is off-limits to everyone else."

"He actually has Unseelie organized enough to handle that? And they don't, you know, try to just break it a little to see what happens?"

"The Fomoire are that serious. No one wants to see that happen. Besides, you've met Peadar's gang. As Unseelie go, they're pretty organized."

"Wait, Peadar? '49ers cap? Desperate need for orthodontia? Tried to kill me?"

"That one," Lani agreed, "He might have even been the one who started referring to the guard shifts as 'going to the lake on a fishing trip.' It certainly wasn't Inwar."

Megan nodded, glancing around. "Okay, that sort of makes sense. I guess he'd be a good guy to have on your side if something did get loose."

They turned away from the eye-lake at last and headed into the hills. "Where are we going, anyway?"

"A little more scouting," Ashling said, her voice unnervingly even. "He hasn't skulked around any of the major landmarks yet, but I want to check all the highlights where he might be crawling around. And then we head for what's next. Probably the tombs."

Lani nodded. "Probably, if he's a treasure hunter. Might have been his whole point of being at the market."

"Might," Ashling said flatly.

"What kind of treasure?" Megan asked.

Lani sighed. "The kind you get by grave-robbing really, really old stuff."

"What, is the acid-eye giant buried here?"

"No. The Fomoire rallied and pulled their own tricks enough that the body was never found after the battle. But it wasn't just Balor here. He had a whole army with him. All of his officers died here, and they were buried, hidden and warded. Sealing them away with all of their stuff was part of the temporary truce—very temporary. We have to make sure they're still secure."

"Or what?"

"Even a mortal with ancient spell books—or enchanted cold iron—that knows about Faerie could do a lot of harm."

"Oh," Megan said, "That kind of or what."

The walk took them deep into the hills, before Ashling urged them to stop near what appeared to be a pile of rocks.

"What's that?" Megan asked.

"From what I've heard," Lani explained, "Warded rocks were piled around Balor's battle standard, since no one of Faerie could touch it."

Ashling's face, however, had managed to grow even colder and more masklike. "But..." she said.

Cassia wasn't as grim, but she was clearly not happy. "Yeah, I know. I've been here with Ric. Pile's all wrong." One leather boot struck out and kicked the pile, which collapsed with nothing inside it. "Our potential burglar's gotten started."

"Then I'd suggest we do the same," Justin spoke up. "Beginning with right near the tear on the map, the closest of the little Xs."

Chapter 10: Barrow

"This is just another weird hill," Megan said as they arrived at their destination.

Regaining some small amount of her usual animation, Ashling got off the crow and danced. As she did, an illusion fell away, revealing an ancient stone door into the hillside. "Come on."

It took Cassia and Justin working together to move the heavy door, and both were out of breath by the time it moved. Cassia grinned at the young knight. "Told you I'd help you work up a sweat."

Justin blushed. Megan found herself wondering why Lani didn't, as she often had, jump to defend her other-brother from the usual Cassia harassment. She wondered if she should do it, or if that would give a wrong impression, or how wrong it would be.

Justin seemed about to respond himself when Ashling darted inside. Everyone else scrambled after her. Megan watched as Jude leapt from her pocket as a kitten and hit the interior floor as a leopard.

"I thought that 'bigger on the inside' thing was just for science fiction," Megan said as they wound through passageways.

As Justin carefully slid ahead of Megan, Cassia muttered, "Can't be much further."

It wasn't true. The passages continued to twist and turn, and, had they not been following Ashling's lead—and the magical light the pixie managed to summon up around herself—Megan was sure it would have been far worse. As it was, Ashling was still distractible even in her somewhat grimmer mood, urging the Count into flitting in back and forth patterns. With such erratic illumination in the dark maze, Justin drew the Sword of Light from its scabbard.

Megan saw occasional signs of previous intruders—mostly bits of bone or tarnished bits of metal now—as well as signs of traps that had been triggered. Lani was happy to assure her that grave robbers got what they deserved. Megan was unsure how much of it was indignation at the crime, and how much was her best friend cheering for the remnants of ancient technology vs. the intruders.

"How is anything here supposed to know we're not grave robbers?" Megan asked.

The first sign of something changing was the hair standing up on the back of Megan's neck, followed by an involuntary shudder. Lani apparently felt it too. "Anyone else thi—"

Had Cassia moved any slower, that first, quick movement might have ended in tragedy. The rushing figure's blade swung towards the group. One second, it was just empty hallway with what looked like an opening into a wider space or room a short way ahead, and then he was there. Cassia got her sword out in time to turn the blade, but not parry it entirely, and the blunt side of the sword grazed Lani's forehead, knocking her back into Megan, setting both girls tumbling to the floor.

From there, Megan was able to get some idea of the figure. He was dressed head to toe in ancient armor, mostly leathers and bronze plates, which showed signs of rot and tarnish about the edges but somehow held together even so. A helmet covered his head completely, but green light showed out through the eye-holes. A jet-black cloak swallowed the light around it, helping hide his exact motions and causing him to blend into the darkness. His sword showed none of the wear of his armor, but the blade was odd, made of black metal, of uneven construction. Megan's first impression was that it was simply badly made, before recalling the gates back in Findias, and comments on how hard it was to make sharp blades of unfired iron, but some found it worth the effort anyway—the figure had a fae-killing weapon.

Cassia, true to her nature, went on the offensive, attacking with rapid, short blows, initially driving the armored figure backwards. Not a blow got through, his sword turning each one aside, but it bought them some space. Maxwell followed his mistress, trying to flank the creature, to either get in quick swipes, or create an opening for Cassia. Justin was slightly slower, and the hallway was cramped, but as soon as he saw an opening, he rushed to try to help. Jude crouched against the wall, not fleeing, but apparently unable to move.

Panicked thoughts sprang unbidden to Megan's mind. She caught herself pulling herself backwards down the hall, away from the fight and her friends, and forced herself to stop. The thoughts remained, though, and the chill in the air kept growing worse. Cassia, Maxwell, and Justin were holding their own, but barely. It took all three of them to keep him from going back on offense, and both Cassia and Maxwell seemed hesitant, only Justin showing no hesitation in standing up to the figure in the ancient armor. Lani was still lying on the floor, starting to move again, but slowly.

That's when she noticed the tugging on her sleeve, and Ashling's voice cut through the haze. "Megan, singing. Singing, now!"

Her thoughts were crawling, fighting the instinct to escape to break through to the surface. "Huh?"

"First rule of bardic magic!" Ashling called.

Ashling's original words on the topic snuck through. "Providing excellent protection for your horse?" That didn't seem to apply.

"That's barding. Totally different! You need to help them." Ashling seemed focused. Under the pixie, the Count seemed to be Actively Not Panicking the same way Megan was.

"Help them?"

"Cassia's magic isn't working. He's got cold iron. You can't affect him, but you can help them."

"Inspiration." Megan remembered that part now. She also remembered how the bard song had helped clear away Peadar's paralyzing terror effect. It wasn't all coming naturally yet, and especially not as naturally as playing with the winds and leaves, but she knew how to do it. Her mind seized on a march, rousing, with lots of highs, and she started to sing. The cobwebs started to clear from her mind, and the song got louder as it did.

Justin had never faltered, likely protected from whatever magic was happening by the Sword of Light in his hand, but Megan could see the effect on the others. Jude left the wall, moving opposite his brother to further divide the figure's attention. Cassia and Maxwell fought more confidently, Maxwell lunging in, taking chances with the sword, backing off only at the last moment, while Cassia resumed the rapid blows, finally getting a hit in on one shoulder.

They collectively drove the figure back into the open chamber, and Megan, singing louder and louder, managed to stand and follow closer, until she reached Lani, trying to keep up the song magic going while checking on her friend. Lani sat up, waving her off. Trusting that, Megan approached closer, careful to stay out of the way of the experienced fighters, while still helping them fight off whatever had been hitting their minds and hers.

Once they were out of the crowded hallway, the numbers started to take a greater toll. First, as the figure reacted to Jude, Maxwell got a deep swipe in to one leg. The leather armor tore open, revealing bone beneath, even though the figure appeared to be filling out the armor just fine. Then Cassia's rain of blows impacting the sword put him off-balance, and Jude barreled into a leg, and the figure dropped to one knee. With Cassia keeping his sword occupied with her own, Justin finally got a clean opening, and the flaming sword separated the helmeted head from the neck, with a sudden bright flare of white light accompanying the swing.

Lani, Megan, Ashling and the Count all entered the open chamber while the fighters caught their breath and tended to small wounds. The dusty room was neatly organized, aside from things upset by the moving fight, with two more suits of armor, numerous weapons, and sacks of treasure set about the area. A raised platform had been kept clean, with the surface showing recently disturbed dust. "What is this place?" Megan started, before adding, with a bit more urgency, "And what was that thing?"

"Burial chamber for an officer." Cassia answered the first, not glancing up from tending to the cats.

"And that was a wight." Ashling covered the second.

"Okay, what's a wight?" Megan asked, quickly amending with, "Aside from really creepy. And please don't go into the paint store spiel. I already know ivory from eggshell."

Ashling showed no signs of wandering off on a tangent, taking the skeletal figure, who still filled out the armor better than a skeleton seemed like it should be able to, deadly serious. "Undead."

"So, that guy is some kind of, uhm, creepy-raising-the-dead guy?"

"Not like zombies or vampires or anything. They don't need necromancers or George Romero bringing them back. Wights used to be legends in their time. Warriors, knights, sorcerers, bards, officers, all different. But all big time. The stories told about them have their own kind of magic, and that combines with some of the biggest badasses having the will to decide they're not entirely dead yet," Ashling explained, relatively reasonably for the pixie.

Megan studied the helmet, then the body to which it had been connected. Ashling was still glowing, and Justin still had the sword out, but the light really did seem to falter more near the body—specifically, as Megan adjusted it, the black cloak. "So, is he actually dead this time?" she asked. "And with all of that, why would he just hang out down here if he was so badass?"

Ashling rode the count up onto the platform, which Megan now figured was where the body was laid. Then the pixie continued. "Because not enough people remembered who this guy was. Undead need food too, but not, like, broccoli and ice cream. Zombies need necromancers helping, vampires need blood, and some of the Senate need the votes of their constituents. Wights are sort of like the popular high schoolers: they need their clique acknowledging their awesomeness. So, back in the day, this guy was famous. Then people forgot his name, and he went to sleep."

Megan listened as she continued fidgeting with the ultra-black fabric. "So, did we disturb him and get him up, or..." As she looked to Ashling, she absently handed the cloak to Cassia, who was rummaging in her pack.

Ashling shook her head. "That's mummies. Something had to give this guy a kick start."

"Okay, so as long as talking about him won't bring him back, who was he? And what would do that? And, I guess, are there any more?"

"I think a lot of those answers are over here," Lani finally spoke up from where she was standing along one wall with Justin. Megan at first was distracted by something on Lani's face—she must have been trying to treat the injury from the iron sword. Eventually, Megan remembered to listen.

"Lots of inscriptions on this wall," Lani was saying. "I'm guessing they wind around to some of the others, too."

"So what does it say?" Megan asked.

"You'll have to ask Ashling. I don't read... whatever ancient language this is."

Ashling and the Count fluttered over to Lani's shoulder, and the pixie started to read. "The Piercing Eye burns in the deep..."

"Well, that's not ominous," Megan said.

Chapter 11: The Gray Lady

"But the part about 'seven dead pallbearers, far from the corpse.' What does that mean?" Megan pondered aloud. "And if our now-headless guy's one of the seven, why are there only four Xs?"

"We only have half a map," Justin pointed out. "The next closest one is deeper in the swamp, with the footnote that we should watch for wisps."

"Well," Cassia said, "The swamp here is the Gray Lady's turf."

Ashling made a 'hmph' sound.

"We should probably ask her about the place, then," Justin said. "At least see if she's at home before crossing her territory."

"Heck no," said Ashling.

"Ashling," Justin said, "This can't be the first time you've needed to deal with someone you can't stand. You've worked too much in a royal court."

Megan frowned. She wasn't really comfortable with the idea either. Her father's former seneschal wasn't someone who inspired trust in anyone present. Still, Justin's approach to How It Is Done had sometimes come through for him in the past. She looked to Lani, who nodded, apparently deciding to back her Other Brother.

"I guess we can try," Megan said.

Ashling frowned more.

"Caw, caw."

"I guess you're right, Count," the pixie said with a sniff. "If they're going, we need to keep an eye on them." And she led the way into a more tree-dense section of the swamp. The ground sloughed further under their feet.

Eventually, the steady flapping pace of the Count's wings changed as he hovered more in place.

"There," Ashling said. "But I'm not going to knock."

It took a moment for Megan to realize what she was looking at in the dusk light, given the construction. While many of the trees had wide root networks that rose, in places, above the water, these were exceptional: forming twisting walkways and a foundation. The

trees that rose from them twisted and turned, just as dark, with all
the reaching branches and hollows as elsewhere, but growing
together as natural building materials, forming a grand, if
foreboding palace rising out of the swamp. She had trouble
imagining the kinds of sorcery that might have gone into building
it—or rather getting the trees to grow and twist just so. "Wow...
that's... kind of creepier than I'd imagined. Which is saying
something."

"Just wait," Cassia said. "I've been here with Ric before. If
she lets us in—big if—there's going to be what looks like a stick and
a primitive hula hoop on the floor. Do not move those. There'll be a
doll on the table. Don't mess with it."

"I don't mess with everything," Megan said defensively.
"But how do you know stuff is going to be on the floor or the
table?"

"You know how some grieving families leave a kid's room
just the way he or she left it?"

"Yeah..."

"The Gray Lady's like that about the whole house. Even
when she's moved, over the millennia, all the kid's stuff gets put in
the exact same place."

Megan stepped up towards the door and knocked. There
was no answer. She waited several moments, and knocked again. "Is
anyone home? We could use some help."

This time, she thought she saw a flicker of pale blue light,
but the small viewing window in the door was above her eye level,
more suited to the taller sidhe than most teen girls. She stood on her
tiptoes, leaning against the door to try to get a better look. It was
still not a perfect view, but she was more certain now that there was
one of the will o' wisps hovering near the door. That was still no
proof but strongly suggested that the Gray Lady might be there.
"Hey, I'm sorry to disturb you," she tried. "But this might be really
important."

She was still met with silence.

"Give me the map," Megan finally called, reaching for it. After Cassia passed it over, she held the map up to the window. "Do you know anything about the wights buried in these spots?"

The pale blue light intensified, and an answer came back in a whisper. "I don't use their names."

Lani stepped closer, nodding firmly. "Darn right. They can just be nobodies... well, except, someone isn't leaving them as nobodies. We just ran into one that woke up. And someone might have Balor's banner."

The door opened without any sign of the Gray Lady's hand or any other. A will o' wisp floated just inside. It began retreating further into the poorly lit home once Megan stepped across the threshold, followed by the others.

The home was just as Cassia had described it, with a variety of simple toys and other artifacts of a small child's presence scattered about the floor, which was otherwise bare, as were the walls, save for the occasional torch. These, Megan quickly found, were similar to some of the magical lights in Faerie, providing light, though very little in these particular cases, but without actually burning down, or giving off much heat. Indeed, despite the flames, the building's interior was colder than the air outside.

The wisp finally led them to the Gray Lady, sitting alone in a large chair in a library room, which finally broke the trend of the rest of her home, furnished in reasonable comfort, with every inch of the walls lined with the kind of books Megan usually associated with words like tomes or grimoires. The will o' wisp floated over to the pale sidhe lady, looking almost like a well-dressed marble statue, for the perfection of her blank features—perfect, that is, aside from the tarnish on her silver hair, the black curves under her eyes, and the shimmering, interwoven lines on her cheeks.

"Hello again, Megan," came the whisper, originating from the will o' wisp. "You mentioned the wights?"

Megan considered trying to find a seat, then just stepped up closer to the sidhe lady, holding up the map. "So, you knew about them?" It sounded dumb to Megan even as she said it: of course the

Lady would know. Megan just assumed wights were the sort of folk the Gray Lady occasionally had over for tea or something.

"Some of them, yes," came the whispers. "I remember some of them from their breathing days. That one in particular." The Gray Lady finally moved just enough to point towards the X within the deepest areas of swampland.

"Oh, well, good. What can you tell us about him? I mean, we handled the one, even when he sort of took us by surprise."

Then Cassia spoke up. "We got lucky. He was just waking up. Burial chamber was barely disturbed."

The comment from the usually cocky satyress caught Megan off-guard enough to turn away from the Gray Lady and give Cassia a quizzical look instead. "Is that going to matter that much?"

Cassia shrugged cheerfully. "Depends. If the kick-start was a one-time thing, they'll wander home and go back to sleep on their own. But if this collector has a cult, or knows the right rituals or something..."

"Then what?"

"Then we're going to have a hell of a fight on our hands. They'll just keep getting stronger, the more time they have to remember who they were."

"Just so," the whisper added, bringing Megan's attention back to their hostess. "And all of them are different." She gestured to the map. "This one was a sorcerer in life, as were many of his followers. His tomb is not warded only by puzzles and gadgets."

"So you heard about him, back when, you know, he was alive?" Megan asked.

"I fought against him in life, when he was allied with the Fomoire, when he was esteemed enough among mortals that many of the Fomoire even knew his name."

Megan didn't know a lot about the Fomoire, but it didn't sound good. "So, Justin's sword is pretty good against magic, and Ashling is good at getting into places, but..."

"But you're not going to be cautious this time, either. You'll investigate, one way or another. So perhaps you'll let me help you?" the Gray Lady offered.

"You must really hate this guy, if you fought him before, and you want to come help us, uhm, re-kill him."

"Not that kind of help. If Balor's banner has been moved, then other parties must be told, and I need to look into other matters."

"But you just said—"

"That I would help you, and I will." She gestured to a spot further north on the map. "His tomb is well guarded by traps and sorcery, but it wasn't warded against the encroaching marsh. Water and tree roots have eaten into the barrow hill. Cassia may be too large, but the rest should be able to climb through the deep roots, and enter the hall the hidden way. Follow the trickle of marsh water and unworked tunnels, but use a minimum of light. You will need surprise, and your wits. If he is, indeed, stirring, then he's dangerous—as the other five will be."

"Five, but... did you know about the writing?"

"All of the tombs have plenty of writing, but I'm assuming seven wights, because of the shroud."

Megan looked back at Cassia. "His cloak? I knew it was magical, but—"

"Powerful magic. It and six like it shielded Balor Birugderc's poison eye, before the storm god killed him. I couldn't mistake it."

Megan trailed behind the others as they headed back into the swamp, with Ashling, Cassia, and Justin debating the best way to go about reaching the hidden way into the barrow. The Gray Lady accompanied them as far as the door. Megan almost thanked her, before recalling how opposed the bane sidhe lady had been to her efforts to rescue her father.

Instead, it was the Gray Lady, via her will o' wisp, who spoke first. "How is he?" came the small whisper.

"Oh, uhm, Dad? He's all right. He's been fretting about, well, not having anyone doing your job." Megan wasn't about to apologize. The Gray Lady had never even tried to contradict Megan's concern that she'd been involved in planning the ambush on her father. She'd just walked out without any effort to defend

herself, so she at least knew something. If that wasn't enough—
which, since Megan had only just acquired her father, it was—
Ashling didn't trust her, and so far, the pixie had been the best
guide to Faerie politics that Megan had.

"I see," came the whisper. "Be careful. And remember, your
magic may not be up to that of a sorcerer's, but if your lessons have
gotten that far, your counter-magics may help."

"I've learned some, yes," Megan asserted, trying to recall a
few of the lyrics Ashling had helped her with, just to assure herself
she could bring the right songs to mind quickly. "We'll be fine."

"We can hope."

The two spent a few moments looking at one another in
silence, Megan questioning the woman's sincerity as to just what
she hoped, and not quite able to bring herself to offer a more
genuine thanks due to those doubts. The Lady, in turn, didn't offer
any more genuine well wishes. After several awkward moments,
the Lady turned, and she and the wisp disappeared back into her
home, the doors creaking shut behind them.

Chapter 12: Backfire

The Gray Lady had been right about a number of things. The tree roots had burrowed into the barrow right where she'd indicated, opening a sort of passage deep into the earth. Likewise, she'd been right on the dimensions. It was a tight fit for Justin and would have been entirely impossible if he'd brought his chainmail.

For Cassia and her broad shoulders, there was no chance, even had she, as she said, "stripped down and oiled up." The offer had received quick, polite refusals. She agreed to stand guard and make sure nothing came in behind them—and gave the cats firm instructions to help out and obey Megan.

Justin kept the sword sheathed this time, since he needed both hands to climb among the roots, and it would have been far too bright. Ashling provided a light source again, at a far lower intensity than before. Back at full size, Maxwell went first, having the easiest time climbing among the muddy, slippery root network, while also having little difficulty with the darkness. Jude stayed near Megan and Lani, providing a rear guard of sorts that wasn't bothered by the darkness.

Eventually, after far too many scratches, slippery mud-near-slides, nearly getting stuck (more a problem for Justin than anyone else), and the uneven light around other climbing people, the path started to level out. For some time, it was still a matter of climbing through tree roots, nearly skating down muddy drops, or figuring out where sinkholes were, but at least it was climbing and clambering forward instead of mostly down.

After what seemed to Megan like an hour of slow, careful walking and occasionally squeezing through tree roots, they reached the first artificial support. The walls started showing fewer signs of encroaching roots, and the earth appeared more worked.

Not long after that, Ashling stopped them. "We're getting close. It's warded. I'm not finding a way around it."

Megan recalled the pixie's occasional very precise movements in the tomb before, and wondered just how many traps she'd allowed them to avoid, beyond those she'd seen evidence of. "So what now?"

"Two options," Ashling responded. "Three if we had a handy backhoe and a three-foot-thick concrete barrier."

"That bad?" Megan couldn't help but ask.

"Only if we cross this line," Ashling pointed out an imaginary line on the floor, "Or mess with the ward the wrong way, or mess up with anti-magic, or maybe jump around too much, or breathe really hard in this direction." Megan and Jude both drew back a little, careful to direct their breath elsewhere, in case.

"So, we have two options. How do we get through?" Megan asked.

"The more I think about it, the more options we have. It's too bad we don't have a goblin minesweeper or something."

"That's a thing?" Megan knew she was going to regret asking, but had to know now. "What sort of equipment do they use for that?" After seeing the goblin market, Megan was trying to imagine what sort of tech or magic might be involved.

"Running shoes," Ashling answered cheerfully. "Hopefully really good ones."

Megan blinked, horrified. "Why would they do that?"

"Ogres, trolls, and redcaps are usually scarier than land mines and runes of warding," Ashling responded with a shrug.

"We're not doing it that way," Lani stepped in. "You started with two options. What are those?"

Ashling sighed. "Okay, so with what we have on hand, I can point out where the wards were inscribed, and Justin could smash it—while we hope the sword's anti-magic is enough—or I can help Megan counter-song them."

"Those are really noisy options," Lani said.

"They're what we have," Ashling said, slightly apologetic. "At least we're close. If we'd gone the other way, this probably would have been right at the start."

"All right, I'll take this one," Justin said.

"You're sure?" Lani asked. "Megan might be safer."

"I'm sure. Counter-magic might be safer, but slower. If this is our chance for surprise, we need to be quick. I'd rather chance this than giving the wight too much time to prepare. And we'll need her soon enough. Everyone but Ashling, back up."

There was some hesitation, but eventually, everyone backed away. Ashling stayed on Justin's shoulder, assuring the Count she'd be fine, then pointed out the spot on the wall where the warding enchantment originated.

The sword struck the wall, and there was instantly two flashes of bright light: the sword's whitish flames and an unnatural green from the wall. Accustomed to the dark, Megan shielded her eyes, but not in time. She was vaguely aware of a lot of motion around her, but could only see swirls and spots. A few moments later, the shouting began, and she heard a ringing of metal on metal, followed by the sound of the cats growling and hissing, followed by more metallic noises.

Something grabbed at Megan's leg, and she almost kicked out, trying to get it away, before Ashling's voice cut through the chaos, and she became aware the pixie was climbing her, shouting something. After a moment to collect herself and focus, the words started making more sense. "Counter-song, Megan, now! They need help!"

Her vision started to clear. The swirls and sparkles started to turn into shadowy outlines. She was pretty sure that was Justin's shadow, fencing with two bulky figures with swords. Leopard-shaped shadows darted in and out of a fight with a couple more of the suits of armor—because as things took on a more coherent shape, she figured out that's what the sources of all the metallic noises were: four suits of ancient armor, without any sign of the men underneath. A fifth figure stood in the background, guarded by the others. This one wore less armor, but seeing more than that was made difficult by—in addition to the lights swimming in front of Megan's eyes—the fact he wore another of the light-eating cloaks. She could, however, see the glowing green of his eyes.

She first hit on the inspirational march from last time, but that didn't seem quite right. Her allies weren't struggling with fighting off fear this time. Still, it couldn't hurt, and it was the first thing that came to mind.

"Not that one!" Ashling called, reaching Megan's shoulder, and starting to hum. Megan caught on, and set into a new song, trying to remember the old Gaelic lyrics by rote memory, rather than actually understanding what she was singing. As she did, Ashling joined in, singing into her ear to help.

As the song started, the wight hesitated, gesturing and moving less, and focusing in on her. As Megan's song echoed through the halls, and the wight's attention shifted, she noticed a marked difference in the armored figures. Their movements were slower, and their swings had less force behind them. Where before, Justin had been struggling defensively, he easily parried a blow aside, and got in a good counter-offensive, leaving a deep cut in one suit of armor. Unfortunately, it didn't fall, as any living combatant would have, but the wound still slowed it down, and left it vulnerable.

The cats, working as a team, were also able to take advantage. When a sluggish swing missed Jude, Maxwell pounced at a knee, knocking the suit over entirely, but he had to back away when the other suit near them lunged. Regardless, the difference in the fight was showing already.

That's when the wight's tactics changed as well. Megan caught hints of a booming voice, speaking some variation of Gaelic, and his right hand began to glow, before he pointed at her, and a burst of bright green fire shot her direction. Ashling's tone in her ear abruptly shifted, and Megan tried to match it... and went silent.

Justin leaped into the way of the jet of fire, with far better reflexes than Megan could have managed. The Claiomh Solais flashed a bright white when the green flames hit. Justin was left lying on the floor, showing no signs of the horrible burns Megan was envisioning, but was still slow to get up, while the armored figures closed on him.

Meanwhile, letting the armored figures move, more slowly, but with less of his direct input, the wight was chanting again, with the fire building back up. Megan made another attempt at the part of the song Ashling was trying to guide her through, but there was nothing. She started to panic, finding that she not only couldn't hit the notes, but when she tried, she went dead silent.

Lani rushed into the breach while Justin was trying to recover from the saving dive, and being hit by whatever part of the spell the Sword of Light hadn't canceled. Lani had a wrench in one hand, and a hammer in the other—neither was proving very effective, but with the armored figures moving so slowly, she was managing to protect Justin, while the cats went back on the defensive.

Just as the next blast of fire was being launched, a small, dark, feathered shape dove for the wight's eyes. Throwing an arm up in front of his face to fend off the Count, the blast shot upward, hitting the ceiling above Megan. The black scorch mark on the stone was bad enough. Much more disturbing was the way the edges of the burn seemed to keep moving, sending black lines snaking out across the stone. Whatever the wight was launching at her, it definitely wasn't normal fire. She kept trying, her mouth moving, but ended up just managing a few orphan notes around gaps of silence. The only thing she was managing was keeping the wight's attention on her, instead of directing the armored figures.

A third blast of fire arced her way, and she jumped to the only song that came to mind, switching to a rock song she'd practiced in her back yard, and sending a blast of wind outward. As she did, she felt Ashling contributing some kind of magical push of her own. The green fire exploded outward on impact with the sudden wall of wind, and she felt an intense blast of heat, followed by a growing nausea. The arms she'd thrown up in front of herself defensively had bright red burns, and given the feel of it, she suspected her face did too.

When she tried to go back to singing, and getting the winds to pick back up, she found that her throat felt raw, and the notes wouldn't come out right. She'd saved herself once, but it wasn't going to happen again.

Thankfully, it didn't have to. As an armored thing closed on Lani, Justin rose to a knee and swept his sword low. It didn't react nearly in time, and the flaming sword took a leg off at the knee, and cut halfway into the other. While the suit kept crawling, it couldn't swing effectively, and Lani fended the other one off.

Maxwell leapt directly over a sword swing from another, attaching himself to the figure's helmet, latching on, and kicking the figure's chest and stomach hard with clawed back legs. While it staggered, Jude raced between the armored legs, springing at the wight as he was about to launch another stream of green flame. The spell hit the wall as the wight fell backwards, with a helmeted leopard clawing at his face.

Justin quickly took out the legs from the figure attacking Lani, freeing them both to rush the wight. The undead figure bellowed a new syllable, amidst trying to protect its head, and both Jude and Lani went flying back as if struck by some sort of wave of impact.

Justin staggered, but the Sword of Light flashed again, and he kept his feet. Regaining his momentum, he took two more long strides and swung, just as a new blast of the green flame was building around the wight's arm. Justin's strike was faster than the spellcasting, burying the sword in the wight's shoulder with all the momentum he could put into the swing. The sword flashed bright again, and the greenish flare died out. The spellcasting in Gaelic was drowned out by a horrendous scream that shook the cavern.

The sword flared again, and the fire seemed to direct itself into the wound. As Megan watched, the wight's green eyes were replaced by a flash of white light, and then went dead. The wight remained still as Justin pulled the sword free, and the other armored figures—both the crawling pair and the two trying to corner Maxwell—fell, lifeless.

Chapter 13: Recovery

Megan's voice cracked a little as she as she slumped, then sat down against the wall, her latest attempt at singing having failed for the moment. But now it was just the pain and hoarseness, not like before, with the sheer silence seizing her throat.

Lani passed her a canteen of water, because of course she had canteens of water, for reasons of Lani. Everyone else gathered around, slumping or lying down in similar states of injury and fatigue, though everyone was at least able to walk under their own power.

"Remember to drone a little on the Ms and Ns," Ashling said. "That always helps in these old-style songs. And don't try to get loud. You'll just strain yourself, and it won't help."

Megan drank, and then nodded. After a few more sips and a few more breaths, she started in again on the healing song. Some of the exhaustion faded, along with the magic taking the worst of the pain from the burns. Megan kept singing, between water breaks.

When she'd fully caught her own breath, and let the minor healing effects take her own edge off, Lani slid closer to Megan, speaking quietly, "So, what happened? You were doing great, and then..."

"I don't know," Megan answered, pausing the song, and taking another drink. "I was doing fine, really starting to feel it working, and then the song was just gone."

"Gone? Like, how?"

Rather than trying to explain, and seeing no harm to the effect, Megan started singing. The first few notes went over fine, and then her voice just disappeared, just as it had during the fight. Then she moved on, the song coming back, before disappearing again.

"That's really weird."

"...Yeah," Megan said, her eyes slowly widening as her mind came together more. "Oh."

"What is it?" Lani asked.

"It's the F#. I can't sing F#. Not in any octave. The doctor meant that really literally."

"The doctor? At the market?" Lani groaned. "Megan, you didn't."

"I did. But how does that even work?"

"It doesn't matter how it works. The important part is that it does. You traded it away and might never get it back. Which, among other things, means those songs are never going to work."

"Among other things?"

"I'm just saying, Megan, you need to be more careful. The things faeries consider to be commodities, you—well, you just need to be careful."

"Okay, I get that this is bad. We're fighting magical undead things. But is there some other commodity that's really getting to you?"

"Well, yes, okay? There is. Mack."

"I'm not going to trade your brother for anything, Lani."

"I know, I just ...He's a collector's item, you know? Humans and other folk having kids is one thing. The same two staying together long enough to have a second ten years later is a unique rarity. A bright, energetic little rarity that thinks everything is awesome, and daisy-chain necklaces are against the first-grade dress code, because I've asked, and I just ..."

Megan reached over and hugged Lani. She wasn't used to seeing the more focused girl talk this quickly and disjointedly. Lani seemed more worked up now than by the fact that they'd almost gotten killed. "I know the stories aren't just stories," Megan said carefully. She'd certainly learned a lot since making '80s-movie baby-stealing jokes, and now she was pretty sure she'd avoid doing it again. "And I guess, yes, I wasn't very careful with that note. But I'm not going to let anyone hurt your brother, okay?"

Lani looked miserable, but hugged Megan back.

Megan kept an arm around Lani, and Ashling and the Count settled in to try to offer some comfort as well. Jude, limping and favoring one back leg, joined not long after. Megan continued the healing song, slowly feeling her own burns getting less intense, though they didn't fade entirely, while the others started showing more signs of life and wanting to move again. From her practice sessions, she was fairly certain healing was never going to be a strong point, but at least she could usually rest and focus while doing it.

After resting, Justin settled in next to the others, lifting away a portion of his burned t-shirt, to show a slight wound. Far more troubling than the faint burn mark, though, were several short, black lines extending out from it. Occasionally, one seemed to move just slightly. "I didn't think it was more than a minor injury, but..."

Ashling gestured to the Sword. "Press that against it."

There was a hissing noise as Justin did what she asked. When he drew the sword away, his skin was undamaged by the contact with the flaming sword, and the black marks had disappeared, leaving only a clean cut in the skin. "What happened?"

Ashling spat. "Fomoire magic. For some of them, just throwing around fire, or lightning, or poisonous slugs wasn't enough. They had to make sure that the survivors had parting gifts."

"Poisonous slugs?" Megan couldn't help but ask.

"Egypt trademarked a lot of the snake magic, so they improvised," Ashling answered, matter-of-factly.

"Of course they did. And I guess, for Justin, the sword is faster. What about the rest of us?"

Ashling frowned. "Well, some of you could borrow the scabbard and sword for a little bit. It might work okay, since you're only half-fae. And then there's antidote magic."

"Does that come in a bardic variety?"

"Well sure, but..."

Megan frowned. "Don't tell me that it's only for Romanian bards, or you need to buckle it on your horse the right way, or something weird. This is serious."

Ashling sighed, turning away to ruffle the Count's feathers, and Megan instantly regretted the comment. Ashling had just started reverting back to more typical responses, after all of her anger at the Butterfly Collector. "I'm sorry."

Ashling looked back and nodded. "I know. That's not it. The problem is, that song has some F Sharps, too. I only know the one. Fomoire magic is nasty stuff. Only so many ways around it."

"Oh." It was all Megan could come up with.

The climb back up was no more fun than the way down, but they ultimately decided that it beat trying to make their way through more magical traps. At least this time, they were able to light their way, and had Justin lead the way with the sword, cutting through branches and roots as necessary.

"So?" Cassia asked, once she verified that everyone, particularly both cats, were safe, beyond Jude's limp.

"He's dead. Or re-dead, or something," Megan volunteered, lifting the shroud they'd taken off the body. She explained the wards and the battle with the suits of armor. "So can we not fight any more undead sorcerers, maybe?"

"We probably shouldn't be fighting any more undead anythings," Lani said. "We've gotten lucky twice. We should go tell your dad and let the experts handle this."

Cassia frowned. "You have an expert. You have the Claiomh Solais... and Sir Shyness there isn't too bad with it. We should do this."

Ashling chipped in, "And this is all we have to find the Butterfly Collector. He's behind this. We have to hurry."

"Why? Sure, he likely has a lot to do with causing the wights to stir, but is that even his intent? We can't exactly question them. What do we have to gain?" Justin said, getting a nod from Lani.

"Caw. Caw"

"The Count says that we might find more information that could hint at what he's up to."

"And anyway, the longer we give them, the stronger the wights are going to get. We need to catch them while they're waking up and still getting reoriented," Cassia said.

"They looked pretty awake to me. That last guy had a lot of magic flying around," Megan said.

"And it would have been a lot worse if he'd had time to, say, enchant those guys with any kind of real commands, instead of puppeteering them, or to set a couple more traps and wards. These were the biggest badasses Balor could find among mortals, back in the day. I say we kill as many as we can now. Then we go brag about it to Ric... that'll get his attention and get him on the case of hunting down the rest of 'em a lot faster than going and saying we couldn't hack it."

"The problem is, maybe we can't," Lani said. "Like I said, we're getting lucky. A crew of redcaps or sidhe knights won't need luck. Yes, these guys are dangerous, but they don't have their armies this time. And they were mortals. Yes, Justin is good. Yes, we're pretty resourceful. But half of us aren't really combatants. This is serious. We need to get bigger guns in on it."

"Bigger guns will take time," Cassia said. "Especially Unseelie big guns. I suppose you could always go to Orlaith. At least she'll take anything Fomoire seriously."

"I don't care if she takes it seriously," Ashling replied. "She'll screw it up, or try to take advantage of it."

Justin looked to Megan. "Whichever way you want to go," he said. "I'll fight for you and do my best to protect you. But I'd counsel going to your father. This isn't safe."

Megan sighed, and looked at Justin, then Lani. "I know this isn't safe. I know we probably should go back to my dad. But it does kind of feel like we need to hurry here. I say we keep going. But we'll try to be careful. We need to try to find this guy, though. After that, if we can figure out who he is, or where he is, we focus on that, and leave the wights to Dad, Inwar, whoever, okay?"

With the concessions made, Lani elected not to argue further. "All right, so where's the next one on the map?"

Chapter 14: Rigged

The next of the barrows turned out to be some distance, but at least it got them out of the worst of the marshy, slippery ground. Maxwell was walking again, exploring at times as they traveled, but Jude continued to favor one leg and to let Megan carry him, at least until they reached the actual barrow.

This time, there was no hidden entrance, just a heavy stone door, long since sealed up. It took Cassia and Justin working together to get it open, and even then, took quite a while to move it. Ashling and the Count took the lead, but Ashling paused only a few feet in, having the Count perch in an alcove that had once held a torch. "I'll do my best, but this place is really warded. Trying to find a safe path through here is kind of like trying to find a haystack in a needle factory."

Megan blinked. "You mean a needle in a haystack?"

Ashling shook her head. "I meant what I said. If you're in a needle factory, there are no haystacks. And if there is one, it's probably a trick. Someone took some time putting some seriously long-lived wards in here. I suspect there's plenty of other traps too."

Cassia, as the most durable, took the lead, with the Count and Ashling each perched on a shoulder, doing their best at guidance. Ashling guided them around a tripwire and around the trigger for a deadfall but missed the poison needle trap. Cassia's armor deflected most of it, but three needles stuck into her skin. Lani immediately set to removing them, and trying to discern what was on the needles, but Cassia, after a moment, shook her off. "It'll be fine. Stings a bit."

"But the poison..." Lani started.

"Satyr," Cassia said, starting to move again. "This is no worse than a really heavy pub crawl on Cap Hill."

Lani and Megan glanced at each other, then moved to follow Cassia. It wasn't all that long before Ashling called them to a halt again, having the Count take her to a specific spot on the floor.

"Okay, everyone, watch carefully. Cassia, you're taller, so you can get the good cereal on the high shelf. And also stand in back so they can see." The pixie dismounted. "There's a hollow floor there, and there, and there. Just step on the spots I step on." Ashling made a huge leap from one floor stone to another, then another one. Megan tracked which she landed on, and took careful steps across.

"Great," Ashling said eventually. "Now not one step closer until Lani deals with this thing right here."

Lani looked. "Yeah, the markings look like it might be another deadfall, but covering the whole hallway."

"It's going to be hard for us to find enough space to sleep," Megan said.

Lani rolled her eyes. "I can at least try to see about dismantling millennia-out-of-date technology before worrying about having to use magic."

She knelt and peered at the wall for a few moments before Cassia just smashed away a thin portion of the stone. "That should make your life easier."

"Huh," said Lani. "It wasn't a deadfall at all. It's some kind of elaborate spike trap. Just when you think you know what to look for..."

"Whoever designed this place was seriously paranoid." Megan said.

"And clever," Justin added. "Most of these don't stand alone. For most people, avoiding one of them would lead you right into the next."

Lani finished her work disabling the trap. "I'd really, really appreciate studying this place, if it weren't trying to kill me."

"We're almost there," Ashling said, starting to move again.

"Better than GPS," Lani said. "And works underground."

"Through that door," Ashling said a few turns and twists later, pointing to another heavy looking stone door. She paused in looking it over, shining brighter. "They're not even trying to hide the wards on this one." Indeed, the door was heavily marked with twisting symbols.

"Easy enough to deal with that," Cassia snarled, smashing the door to mar the symbols, not giving Lani or Justin time to shout a warning. As she hit it, the floor fell away from under them.

Most of the group hit the stone floor beneath heavily. The cats seemed to have a better time landing on their feet, while the Count managed to lift off and grab Ashling before she hit the ground. Cassia was back on her feet in an instant, the teenagers took more time about it. No one was able to get out before the former floor, now their ceiling, closed again some fifteen feet above their heads.

"I'm sorry!" Ashling called, brushing herself off and starting to scan the room, which had no signs of any doors, or much of anything but bare stone, and some darker stains on the floor, amidst a few flat bits of metal and fragments of bone. "I don't know how I missed that one."

"It's okay, Ashling," Lani said, "The wards were probably about hiding that, not protecting the room. Another trick. We just need to figure out how to..." She paused as a grinding noise echoed around them. "Uhm, how to stop the walls from closing in on us. That's probably more immediate than getting out."

The walls didn't move especially fast, but were definitely moving. Cassia's efforts to push back made no difference, likewise, even with the Sword of Light, and the satyr's strength, the walls resisted efforts to do more than scratch them. Cassia seemed to feel only slightly better about this when Lani suggested that the wards probably had something to do with that, too.

Seconds passed, with the walls continuing to grind. Megan, and even Ashling made efforts to help with the pushing, while Lani studied the edges, looking for flaws or gaps. She finally found a couple points where the stone had worn down, but wasn't able to do much with it, and the gaps turned out to be much too small for even Ashling to fit through.

Just as it was getting hard to breathe in the cramped space, Justin jammed the Sword of Light between the walls, and the indestructible sword turned out to be good to its reputation, holding them apart just enough for people to stand, and move slowly, though Cassia, and, to a lesser degree, Justin, had to squeeze a little, and only the cats, the Count, Ashling, and Lani had any hope of getting past anyone.

"What now?" Megan finally asked.

"One of three things," Lani responded, trying to use the time to continue searching the walls for anything that might help, "Either the mechanisms pushing the walls break down, we run out of air, or..." she gestured to where the tip of the sword had begun being driven into the wall, despite its resistance, though barely perceptibly so far, "Or the sword eventually gets pushed in like a nail, and we get flattened anyway."

"I don't like those odds. Ashling, you open stuff all the time. Can you do that here?"

"One, wards, big ones. Two, that's windows and stuff. If I had a dozen pixies here, sure, but..." she went very quiet.

Megan spent a few moments looking around, finally settling on Lani, "Can you figure out how to shut it down?"

"In theory, with enough things to make the right tools from, and time. But not while you're all awake."

"But you could do it if you had some stuff to work with, and we were sleeping?" Ashling asked.

"Sure, probably. Menehune thing. But I think everyone is a touch high stress. And if anyone wakes up, I'm done."

Ashling pointed to Cassia. "Give her your breastplate. Spare metal bits. Anyone have candles?"

Cassia started in on removing the armor, while Lani dug into her bag, and offered up two candles, looking confused. "Those are good to have in emergencies. This better be important, though. I was serious about running out of air."

"Very important," Ashling responded, setting up the candles with some help, and having Lani light them. "We can't have you falling asleep. Everyone but Lani, get as comfy as you can." When Lani continued to look confused, but spent time laying her tools out anyway, the pixie continued, "I'm going to help Megan with a lullaby."

"Cool!" Megan replied, despite the situation, "Anti-magic, wind and cold stuff, inspiration, healing, and now putting people to sleep? Is there anything bardic magic doesn't do?"

Ashling gestured up, "Absolutely terrible for stopping stone wall traps."

"Point taken."

Finally, Ashling seemed content with the candles, collecting hot wax and rolling them up, offering it to Lani. "Ear plugs."

Everyone settled as best they could, and the pixie started to guide Megan through a new song. It took a while, and as they worked it out, the sword visibly shifted a couple times, pushing into the wall about an inch. Megan did her best to shut out the grinding and focus on learning the song.

At first, she was sure nothing was happening, aside from the sword shifting another half an inch, forcing Cassia to shift again, and leaving things tight enough Lani would have to crawl over people and hope the music was enough to keep them asleep if she needed to get to any other part of the room.

The cats fell asleep first, followed by the Count, and then Justin. Megan felt her own eyelids getting heavy, and did her best to let the song take her too, despite being the one casting. She kept singing when Ashling quieted, going still, using Megan's stomach as a pillow, and then she heard soft snores from Cassia's direction, before Megan drifted off as well.

She was shaken awake by Lani, urging her to hurry. The ceiling had opened, and the walls had moved apart slightly, letting Justin free the sword. Cassia made the fifteen foot leap upward, then held the other end of the rope Lani had drawn from her bag, easily holding on while the others climbed out. "How did you do that?" Megan asked, once they were free, and Lani triggered the floor closing again.

"Sort of a cross between opening a locked car with a coat hanger, and convincing the trap it had closed all the way. Sorry about your armor, Cassia. I needed all the bolts."

Cassia shook her head, "I figured. I can get more made. But if you really want to get my clothes off, Lani, there's easier ways."

Lani sighed, trying to turn her attention to the warded door. "At least you still have a couple layers on. You are wearing a wrap, right?"

"Another death trap or two, or some good wine, and you can find out."

Lani finally found a safe point to stand and had Justin mar the wards with the sword from there. It didn't take long once they were destroyed for Cassia to force the door open.

Inside was a burial chamber much like the others, ornate, full of old treasures—but the body was missing, the dust had been disturbed, and the weapons rack had open spaces where a sword and shield were supposed to be. The room was also full of rolled up parchments. Lani immediately turned her attention to those, while the others looked around.

"I guess he already left. Where do you think he could have gone?"

"These might have some kind of clue, but I'm not sure," Lani said, with one parchment unrolled on the raised alcove where the body had been laying, delicately unrolling another, "I think they're maps, but all marked up. I can't read them, and I'm not sure what all these lines and arrows are."

Cassia perked up, moving to look. "Tactical maps. Ric has a copy of this one, from the perspective of the other side. Guessing this guy is some kind of strategist."

"It would make sense that some of Balor's officers would be," Justin agreed, moving to study the two open maps.

"So after all of that, we just missed him?" Megan asked.

"But we should take these maps, and try the last place on our map and hope for better luck. These are all really old, but they might still give us some clues."

The group packed up as many of the rolled-up parchments as they could and carefully made their way back out of the burial chambers.

Chapter 15: Wandering

"Well," Megan commented as they started to make their way to the very edge of the swamp. "We can't get too negative. The dead-tactician guy might just be wandering aimlessly until he wears out again. We don't know that he's actually going to do anything with the Butterfly Collector." She looked at Ashling with what she hoped was reassurance.

Before the pixie could respond to that, a voice came from somewhere to their left, laced with countertenor giggling. "What are the odds of that, you figure?" Megan and Lani startled, looking in the direction of the noise. Cassia growled low even before she looked, and the cats joined in. Ashling just sighed. "Bother. You had to show up now?"

The figure leaning against the tree looked a little like a middle-school kid, provided that middle school had an extremely lax dress code that allowed long, messy hair and very ragged clothing. A look at his glinting eyes quickly indicated that he really wasn't young at all. Megan quickly remembered to look away. She'd had bad experiences looking some Faerie creatures in the eyes, particularly ones with sardonic smiles.

Cassia said something in Greek that Megan was fairly sure wasn't nice.

"Nice to see you, too, Cass."

"What do you know about all this, Rob?"

"Enough to find it hilarious, obviously. But why should I drop spoilers? Merry wandering!" And with another trill of giggles, he was gone.

"Check the supplies." Ashling suggested automatically. "The sooner we find out what he did, the better."

"Why? Who was that?" Megan asked, even while starting to help Lani, who was already checking their rations and tools.

"Robin Goodfellow," Cassia snarled, checking over her weapon and few other possessions.

"That sounds vaguely English-y familiar," Megan admitted. "Now that I've been at this stuff a while, though, I'm guessing it's more complicated than anybody thinks."

"A powerful faerie. Like, on par with the King and Queen powerful, in his own way. Except he just uses it to cause trouble," Ashling responded. "Except when he doesn't. Those times, when people leave him milk and bread, well, then he weaves a really neat sweater."

"How is that different than... well, a lot of you?"

"Because right now, he's pissing me off," Cassia responded.

"What Cassia means," Ashling said, "Is that no matter how many sweaters he's made someone, the first time he visits and doesn't happen to have been left milk and bread, he's as likely to burn their house down as anything. I mean, don't get me wrong, he's fun at parties, but Rob lives in the moment."

"I said what I meant." Cassia answered.

"I'm still not seeing how that's different."

"Because," Lani finally stepped into the conversation, "Even most of the Unseelie balk at things like messing with the undead, or triggering ancient curses, or playing with things belonging to the Fomoire. If it will cause some chaos, he'll probably do it."

"So why is he messing with us?"

"It's what he does. And he must have pulled something, but all our supplies are in order. The granola's not even stale."

"So let's at least try to catch up with him and find out," Megan said.

They moved for a while, trying to check the area around the tomb for tracks or any other sign of his passage without luck. The leopards perked up a couple of times, but whatever sign there was, it never led anywhere. Likewise, Ashling and the Count circled above, but, much to the pixie's disgust, never had anything new to report when they descended again.

The group finally checked the map and started towards the final tomb listed, slogging over the soft, marshy ground. Megan finally called for a break to catch her breath and rest her feet. Some time later, she called for another, with Lani and the cats in firm agreement.

"It doesn't look that far on the map," Megan said.

"You are moving pretty slowly," Ashling responded.

"Not that slow," Lani said. "We can't all hop on a crow and fly."

"She's right, though," Justin said. "Our destination is no further from the last tomb than the first and second were apart. But it's taking longer this time."

Cassia said, "You're just slowing down because you're tired."

Lani stood staring. She looked at the cats. Maxwell and Jude were both resting next to a tree, occasionally yawning and stretching. "Wait..." Lani said. "Megan, we left the tomb, what, two hours ago?"

"Yeah," Megan said. "So it's probably safe to say by now we're officially lost."

"No," said Lani. "Well, yes, but that's not the point I wanted to address first." She pointed at the leopards. "Why are they still at full size?"

Megan blinked.

"Huh," said Cassia.

Ashling sighed. "So that's what he did: a dreamscape illusion. Robin Freaking Goodfellow. One of his favorites."

"Ok, so I understood illusion. And we haven't gotten out of its range yet? How big of an illusion can he make?"

"That's the point of dreamscape illusions," Ashling explained, happily forgetting her cursing of the other faerie to go into explanation mode. "We've been going in circles. So, you know, they're really excellent for tropical vacations. Get someone who can do them to lay one down, and you have a tropical vacation. Swimming, private beach, maybe nice little house with a view. All in fifteen feet. You know, 'til it ends, and you're in your bikini in Minnesota."

"I don't think this is supposed to be a vacation," Megan said, gesturing to their surroundings.

"Okay, well that's the other point of them: to get people lost or keep them from going anywhere. That's probably it this time."

"Yeah, that's probably it. So how do we get out?"

"It will go away eventually," Ashling explained.

"And how long is eventually?"

"Longer than we have," Lani said. "We need to find another way out. What are our options?"

Ashling considered. "We can look for the flaw in the illusion."

"How do we do that? If he's that good, is there even a flaw?" Megan asked.

"They all have them. The better the illusionist, the smaller the flaws. But eventually, his magic will have gotten bored with it. A tree will repeat, or there'll be the same bird sounds. If the illusion stops working right, and we know it, it's easier to break."

"We know it's an illusion. So it's already not working right," Megan said.

"You want a saving throw? You might know it's an illusion, but your brain is still getting information from your senses. Until you convince them, we're stuck."

"We can't just walk in a straight line?"

"Why, have you been drinking?" Ashling paused. "And not sharing?"

Megan sighed. "If the illusion tricks us into walking in circles, it seems like we should be able to get outside of it if we can stay on track."

"Sure, maybe. If you have something to follow that's not illusion. You can think you're walking perfectly straight, and you've actually been walking without rhythm the whole time."

"Is that some sort of bard thing?"

"The worms like bards just fine, yes."

Megan blinked and looked towards Lani, who sighed, and started looking around again as if she might spot the discrepancy right there.

"Wait, Justin, why aren't you dealing with all this?" Megan asked.

"I beg your pardon?"

"The sword. The magic-cancelling. You busted open the wards. You've cut through magic weapons. A whole murmur of sprites can't zap you. Why are you stuck in this dreamscape illusion thing?"

"If you'll indicate where to slice it open, Highness, I will be happy to follow instructions. Or you might let me have ten years to develop a broader-based understanding of technique, but I am hoping to get you home sooner than that."

They moved a little further, but Megan's feet started to ache again, and she paused to rest, thinking through the situation while the others scanned the area around them further. "Hey, what about the cats?"

"What about them?" Cassia asked, scratching Maxwell between the ears.

"Couldn't they, like, smell something and go find it, or something? They don't rely just on sight the way we... and, uhm, birds do, right?"

"It's worth a try." Lani agreed, then paused to let Cassia and Ashling confirm the plan with the cats. Maxwell was eager to try out being the hero, charging into the trees, while Jude was more hesitant, but duly sniffed the air and started searching the area for a way out. Eventually, Maxwell came charging up behind them, stopping and looking confused, and Jude just circled back to them.

Ashling shook her head. "They're still getting the same cues we are. Having really good hearing and stuff here isn't any more helpful than you having really good eyes."

Megan thought about that a little longer, humming to herself as ideas bounced through her head. She rejected a few, and finally stepped up to Jude, while addressing Ashling again. "So, it's just an illusion, right? We only think we're seeing straight lines, while we're going in circles and stuff, but it's not actually physically moving us around or anything, right?"

"Right. Robin doesn't do that kind of magic. If he wants someone moved, he kidnaps them to a tower in Faerie or something." Lani twitched.

Megan searched until she found a stick and brought it over to Jude, holding it in front of the cat. "Can you smell that?"

Ashling confirmed the movement of Jude's head was agreement. At that, Megan pulled the leopard's goggles down, then covered the lenses with mud.

"Hey, what are you doing? He won't be able to see anything," Cassia said, moving towards Megan.

Lani held a hand up. "I think I understand. That's the point. Make him rely totally on other senses."

Megan nodded, hushing everyone. "He'll need to hear where it falls." she explained, before throwing the stick as hard as she could. As soon as she heard the stick land in the distance, she tapped on Jude's back. "Find it."

The cat took off in the direction of the noise, and, at Megan's urging, the rest of the group followed, taking care to focus strictly on trailing the cat. By the time they found him, the tiny kitten in the leather helmet was playing with the now much-too-big-for-him-to-fetch stick. "I think we're safe." Megan said, crouching to pet the kitten and clean the goggles.

Chapter 16: Beastly and Sacred

After his role in their escape from the illusion, Jude was only too happy to return to Megan's pocket for a nap. With all the extra walking, and discovering that they hadn't made any progress after all, Megan's legs felt like lead, and more than anything, she just wanted a nap herself. Lani looked only a little better off, and the Count was spending far more time resting on Cassia's shoulder than flying. Only the two full faeries looked unaffected.

Megan tried one of her anti-fatigue songs, which seemed to help progress a little, but not nearly as much as she'd have liked. "Much as I don't want another wight alive and moving—or less dead and moving—I kind of hope we don't have another fight on our hands," she said, as they approached the last of the tombs marked on their map.

"Speak for yourself," Cassia grumbled. "After that hassle, I'm ready to kick someone's ass and pretend they're Robin."

As they neared the door to the structure, Jude again jumped out of Megan's pocket, reaching full form along with his brother by the time his back paws hit the ground in front of the tomb.

After checking to make sure the doors didn't have protective runes or other wards against Faerie magic, Cassia and Justin went to work prying the door open. This one came open more readily than the earlier doors they'd had to pry open had. As soon as it was open far enough, Cassia drew her sword and gestured to the leopards. She and Maxwell, followed by Justin and Jude, started forward.

"Wait!" Lani called, but too late.

The doors swung shut again, slamming closed much faster than they'd opened. Justin and Jude darted backwards—though Justin tumbled to the ground in the process—ending up outside, while Cassia and Maxwell were trapped inside the tomb.

Moments after the door closed, multiple figures seemed to melt out of the light tree cover nearby, having been nearly invisible a moment before. An unearthly scream heralded a falcon leading the way, rushing at Lani, who dove to the ground to avoid its talons. A monstrous hound followed. At first, it rushed at Justin, still on the ground, but veered away as the knight managed to draw the Claiomh Solais, shying away from the flaming blade.

The two beasts, each with eyes the same glowing green as the earlier wights, were followed by their apparent master. He was the biggest of the wights yet, wearing only light armor, his skin covered in twisting tattoos, a couple of them glowing faintly green.

The big figure drew a claymore from over his back, swinging down hard at Justin, who barely managed to get his sword up in time to parry. Sparks flew from the Claiomh Solais on impact. Prevented from standing, Justin scrambled back as best he could, keeping his sword up and on the defensive, with the wight following close after.

The doors to the tomb shook with Cassia's obvious efforts to escape. Every time they did, one of the runes on the wight's skin glowed brighter, and Megan guessed it was some magic that allowed him to shut the door, and keep it closed against the satyress's powers, since they hadn't found any enchantment on the door itself. "He's using magic *and* using a sword. That's not fair!" she called to the others.

"We noticed. Can we discuss fair later?" Lani called back, backing away from the advancing hound. As it was about to lunge at her, Jude barreled into its side, unable to knock it down, but at least throwing it off enough that Lani was able to avoid being trapped. The dog turned and snapped at the leopard, who darted back, taking a few scratches from a graze with the undead hound's teeth, but avoiding anything worse from the bite.

After diving at Lani, the falcon quickly engaged Ashling and the Count, the two birds wheeling and darting about in the sky, with Ashling having to hold on tight during the evasive maneuvers. Amidst the attacks, a few black feathers flew, floating down to the ground after each close call.

Focusing purely on defense, with the advantage of the magical sword, Justin was managing to stay alive, but wasn't able to get up or get in any attacks of his own. He was running out of room to keep sliding back. The wight's sword, Megan guessed, had some kind of enchantment of its own, given that it hit the flaming sword repeatedly without breaking.

Considering that and the glowing runes, she started into the counter-spell song, the one Ashling had run her through the most. She was three notes in, almost sure she was seeing the glowing tattoos fade slightly, before she remembered her earlier use of the song, of her throat seizing up. Megan fell silent pre-emptively.

Lani returned the favor to Jude, diving at the monster hound's hindquarters, throwing it off balance as it tried to lunge. Because of her interference, the snapping jaws missed, and it took a claw rake across the face, though that didn't slow it down at all. It whirled, the motion flinging Lani away, sending her tumbling in the grass. Jude got in another slash with his claws, cutting deep into the dead flesh, but it didn't show any signs of slowing down the hound.

The falcon clipped the Count, who floundered, starting to tumble, then managed to pull back up. As the falcon dove to follow up, Ashling leapt off the Count's back, managing to grab onto one of the falcon's wings, changing its trajectory enough to make it miss. The larger bird rose again, with the pixie clinging on tenaciously, trying to buy her mount time to recover.

"Megan, some help!" Lani yelled, backing away from snapping jaws again, as she and Jude alternately tried to keep the hound off balance. Megan started towards Lani, then paused, looking to Justin, trying to figure out whom to help, and how. Everyone was in trouble, and the quickest spells to come to mind were all either less than relevant or less than singable.

Justin was backed up against a tree, fighting as best he could just to fend off attacks from the larger warrior, who was far quicker with the huge blade than he should have been. Still, Justin was managing to keep himself alive and armed despite the heavy blows.

He started to stand, bracing himself against the tree, but ducked back down under a furious swing, hitting the ground as the claymore flashed over his head. Megan guessed he had hoped to bait his opponent—and maybe get the other sword stuck in the tree to create an opening. If so, the effort failed, as the claymore cut right through the tree in a single blow.

Megan remembered one of the songs from the book: a simple one in basic C major—for practical purposes, anyway, since old-style music probably wasn't written with modern musical theory in mind. Megan tried to focus. The point was there were no sharps, no chance at all to sabotage herself. She remembered it had worked, but other songs had worked quicker—and had easier lyrics. With so little practice, she couldn't remember the strange Gaelic words. Th-something? La-something? She tried humming, but there wasn't enough power to it.

The falcon finally shook Ashling off, sending the pixie tumbling, flapping her tattered wings furiously to slow her fall. The Count managed to get under her, aiming his dive in time to let Ashling grab on and swing back into riding position.

Megan had to help now. She knew whom, and she knew how—if this worked. She started to sing the most familiar words that fit the melody, and hoped that Ashling would know the tune, at least. "Thistle, Lavender, Mulberry and Mauve." It was just a selection of pastel shades of pink and purple, but Megan sang it with passion.

Indeed, Ashling seemed to recognize it, as she and the Count flew towards Megan as fast as they could, as the song built up. With the others continuing their desperate battles, all showing the signs of their fatigue, with the close calls getting closer, Megan forced herself to focus on her timing. The falcon saw his targets retreating towards the formerly confused girl and flew after them, picking up speed. As the Count got close enough, Megan caught the pair, holding on as she sang louder. Just as the Falcon's talons closed within inches of her face, a powerful blast of wind blasted it backwards, sending the bird spiraling towards the hound. When it hit the other beast in the flank, accustomed to the other pair attacking every time it focused, the hound whirled and snapped, clipping the falcon before it could dart away.

"Ashling, the door! I'll keep the bird off you."
"Megan, I told you, house windows are one thing. That thing is way too heavy for one pixie."

"Just counteract his closing magic, or whatever. Cassia will do the rest."

The figure with the claymore noticed the surge of bardic magic, buying Justin a moment as the wight considered Megan. Before he could rush her, Justin went on the offensive. The wight fended off the attack cleanly, clearly more than a match in pure skill for the young warrior, but worried enough about the Claiomh Solais that he couldn't ignore the attacks to go stop Megan from grounding the falcon.

While the Count was likewise kept on the ground amidst the magical winds, Ashling was able to drop to the ground and dart towards the door, casting her best opening spells.

The heavy door crashed open a few moments later, and an enraged Cassia barreled out of the tomb with Maxwell at her side. Lani was given a badly needed respite as the two cats teamed up on the hound, letting Lani crawl away to catch her breath and check the severity of the cuts she'd taken so far. Cassia trusted the cats to handle themselves and moved to help Justin, slashing down furiously at the wight. While his skill may have been sufficient to ward off Justin, Cassia was a different matter, and several cuts hit home. The undead shrugged most off, until she managed to lock swords with him, tying up his defense.

A moment later, Justin took advantage, taking the wight's sword arm off at the elbow. A thrust followed, and the flaming sword buried itself in the wight's chest. The green eyes went out, then were replaced by white flames.

With another swing, Cassia took his head off. As soon as he fell, both the falcon and the hound dropped, flesh rotting and crumbling away until both were nothing but skeletons, their animation apparently tied to their master's.

Megan moved towards Lani, and Justin staggered over as well. Finally, they collapsed beside her. All three sat together, trying to recover their breath as Lani continued to check her injuries. The Count slowly hopped over, and the cats lay down nearby. Cassia came to check on them, showing especial concern for Jude's numerous deep cuts from the fight. Ashling set at tiny hand on the Count's wing in tired silence.

Finally, there was a breathless voice. "'Thistle, Lavender, Mulberry, and Mauve'?" Lani asked, an eyebrow raised.

"I didn't exactly have time to check the liner notes in the middle of combat. We don't even have the songbook with us. Anyway, it worked, so those are the words now."

"I can't believe a filked song worked," Lani said.

Ashling shrugged. "It's nothing new. Okay, sure, hers were kind of overly clean by traditional standards, but still..."

Megan was just recovering enough to head back for the wight to collect his cloak, as they had the others, and perhaps get a better look at his sword, when she saw movement.

At first thinking the wight was somehow getting back up, she screamed. Then she recognized the figure crouched next to the body, removing the wight's cloak.

"Robin," Cassia spat, sounding like it was a curse word.

"Don't worry, Cass. Just leaving." he responded with a smirk, tucking the cloak over his arm.

"What do you even want it for?" Megan ventured, holding up a hand to try to keep Cassia from doing anything they'd regret.

"Well, that's a complex question. Why is it wanted? Because apparently to wield sacred power, you need the sacred around—for a very, very *special* definition of sacred. But really, as to why I'm getting it? Just for laughs."

"Sacred? What?" Megan tried, confused.

"Nuh-uh, that's all the clues you get," Robin said. "Goodbye."

Cassia lunged, but by the time she reached him, Robin had either disappeared in a flash of tiny, sparkly lights, or appeared to well enough that the spectacle let him slip away.

Chapter 17: Ice Cream

The walk back seemed to take forever, though Megan's efforts to combat the fatigue with some of her magic helped. There were some efforts to discuss the implications of Robin's words, and what the Butterfly Collector might want, but most were cut off by Cassia's snarling, Ashling's wild suppositions and comments—usually pertaining to the Butterfly Collector's ancestry, preferences, and mental capacity—or, most often, by simple exhaustion.

They emerged back into the noise of the Goblin Market, right near a drink stand staffed by a woman dressed in vines and accessorized with pinecones. As the drinkseller and Cassia exchanged grins and nods, Justin, picking up the bass case from where he'd stashed it there, put the Sword of Light back inside. He had to stop for a minute to rest before hefting the case up over his shoulder.

The Count perched on one of Megan's slouching shoulders while Ashling climbed over to the other. "We need to talk to the king," the pixie said.

"How are we supposed to find him, if he's even here yet?" Megan asked.

"Let's try the picnic area." And Ashling began giving rapid directions to which everyone had to catch up.

Not far from the bazaar was a small grassy field, crowded with the oddest picnic scene Megan had ever seen. Instead of the usual wooden benches, the area was lined with heavy stone tables. The stark gray of the stone was contrasted by the brightly colored umbrellas and canopy tents, many of the latter garishly decorated with streamers, bead curtains, and personal touches that ranged from the silly to the macabre, sometimes in the same tent—such as the canopy adorned with dolls and stuffed animals... and sometimes just their heads, or the tent decorated in what first appeared to be translucent white silks, until one noticed the numerous spiders crawling around on and in the spidersilk curtains. Some of the crowd skipped the tables, settling in the grass, or on blankets, assembling in mixed groups that were every bit as odd as the wild displays.

In the center was laid out a midnight-blue blanket, over which a handful of white-winged sprites fluttered. Megan could see that they were clutching papers, parchments, and what may have been a tiny smartphone. Sitting beneath this chattering whirl, his coal-black hair flowing down over his rough silk shirt, was the Unseelie King, quietly eating ice cream.

"Dad?" Megan asked hoarsely.

He looked up. "Megan! You look exhausted. Come sit down, all of you. Would you like some ice cream, dearest?" He raised his spoon. "The moonlit mist flavor is excellent, but I can also recommend the narcissus."

"I've never heard of those flavors. What are they?"

"Precisely what they sound like. Moonlit mist takes a while to collect, but for those with the palate for it, you can taste Luna's favor. Narcissus is, well, less subtle, but I like it, anyway."

Megan finally settled on the moonlit mist, while Lani stuck to strawberry. Riocard sent a couple of sprites off to place their orders, scrawled on fancy parchment scraps, while the girls settled in.

Once she'd gotten off her feet for a few moments, Megan launched into the explanation of their adventure, though she glossed slightly over the issue of having bartered away a portion of her magically relevant musical capacity. It was embarrassing, and they had a lot of ground to cover. Cassia laid out everything they'd acquired. Ashling explained a few of her slightly more probable scenarios for what the Butterfly Collector might be up to.

Riocard listened to all of this: the chase in the market, the half-map, Mag Tuired, the missing banner, the tombs, the grave-poem about Balor and his 'pallbearers,' the Gray Lady, the wards, the death trap, the tactical charts, Robin Goodfellow, and the stolen shroud.

He listened but never put down his spoon.

"Well done all around," he said pleasantly. "I thank you very much for your work. You should go ahead and keep the shrouds, and I'll look forward to perusing all of the rest sometime when I'm not eating. Would hate to get sticky fingers on historic documents. I'll have them taken to my room, if you don't mind."

"And what about the Butterfly Collector?" Ashling said.

"Let's hope he can be found relatively soon—although part of me would almost prefer that it wait until I've returned to the throne. Orlaith—or Inwar on her behalf—would probably do something unoriginal, like kill him. I'm thinking more of an oubliette." He smiled at Ashling. "That would get him off your mind properly."

"But Dad, there were wights!" Megan said. "And that Robin person!"

"Indeed. I can see the concern. I'm very glad that Cassia and the cats were there, and retaining a knight certainly seems to have been an excellent investment."

"Yeah, we'd have been killed without them. And there might be more."

"Indeed there might be. Having only half a map opens up all sorts of intriguing possibilities."

"Intriguing? This is serious, Dad."

"Indeed it is. I'll send a couple of messages out, see if anyone has heard anything." Riocard scribbled idly on some more pieces of parchment, handed them off to messenger sprites, and returned to his ice cream.

Megan tried a different direction with her questions. "So, the Gray Lady, do you think she might be—"

"—No." Her father actually interrupted her. "Whatever happened between us, she would never be interested in benefiting anyone who would interact with what's left of the Fomoire dregs. She might make many poor choices, particularly revolving around her grief, but she wouldn't abdicate her own nature by helping its source."

Megan glanced at Ashling. The pixie's frown suggested she wasn't any more convinced than Megan was, but she dropped the subject for now. "All right, so now that we know the wights are out there, and the Collector is out there, and Robin is doing—something or other—what do we do now?"

"I just did it. I'll get word out, and we'll look into it."

Moments later, the ice cream arrived. Riocard seemed far more focused on Megan's opinion of it than on the urgent topics she'd brought to his attention.

Megan took a bite. She felt the frozen crystals brush across her tongue and, after a moment, answered her father's unspoken question with, "Yeah, it's good." Annoyed and exhausted as she was, she had to admit it was true. "Refreshing. Of course, I'll have to check, the next time I'm walking through mist in the moonlight, to see if any sticks to the roof of my mouth like this."

That got a rich, dark laugh out of the Unseelie King. "Please do, and let me know. And Lani, wouldn't the ice cream go well with one of your chef friend's shortcakes?"

Lani, never particularly eager to be called on by the king, simply nodded, and Riocard was satisfied.

"In all," he said, "aside from the unpleasantness you've mentioned, the market seems to be going well so far."

Finally, after a bit more small talk with her father, and a couple more attempts to get more urgency out of him regarding the wights, Megan thanked him for the ice cream, and the group stepped away from the picnic area, though Cassia kept glancing away from them, back towards the woman with the pinecones.

Finally, when she decided they were far enough away from Riocard and potential eavesdropping sprites, Lani let her grumbling get a bit more audible. "Aside from the unpleasantness, the market is going well—that's sort of like, 'So, aside from that, how was the play, Mrs. Lincoln?" Then she sighed, and fully spoke up. "Okay, so that wasn't very helpful. What do we do now?"

Megan sighed. "We go home, clean up, and get ready for the concert tomorrow—tonight?" Megan started to get confused about days,

"Tomorrow," Cassia said absently. "Everybody still gets to sleep. Because of string theory or whatever."

"Yes, but…" Lani was staring at Megan. "So…Wait… he's got Balor's standard, there's a bunch of ancient military officers awakening, Robin Goodfellow is running around, and we only have half of the map, if that. And you want to do what?"

"Do you have a better idea?" Megan said.

"Than going back home? Maybe. We need to find him." Lani's comment was met with firm nods from Ashling.

"We will, I just need to think about this. I mean, what did we do last year when we almost had the year without an Autumn?" Megan said.

"Went back to my place and danced around to your mom's old songs," Lani admitted.

"Right, and it worked. Cassia, can you play 'Yet Another Song About Jumping' at the concert?"

"Done."

Chapter 18: Bass

Megan was dropped off in front of her house with weary goodbyes and a flustered wiping at her face once more. As she approached the house, she saw lights on in the front room, and motion from inside.

Even though she hadn't been gone nearly so long as it felt, Megan thought her mother might be pacing about, waiting for her to get home. She braced herself for questions and motherly concern as she opened the door. Instead, she was met by music, specifically, a familiar bassline, accompanied by her mother's voice. For a moment she thought maybe a CD was playing the opening to 'Why is it Monday?,' but there was her mother, on the couch, the orderly coffee table shoved out of the way to make room, plucking the cords on her old bass and singing.

While she sang quietly, her voice wavered more than in the lines Megan remembered, and the lyrics didn't match the liner notes of the original.

"Head to my 9 to 5, / Though it's really 8 to 8. / The band has Van Halen M&Ms, / And traffic's jammedtoNorthgate..."

The end words ran together as her mother tried to make the cadence of her current job difficulties match the pace of the original song. She was wrapped up enough in the composition that she didn't even seem to notice the door open and close, or Megan staring, wide-eyed.

She finally recovered from her surprise enough to interrupt the song, "Hi, Mom. I'm home."

"Hi, sweetheart." Sheila O'Reilly sounded as tired as ever, but ... well, Megan was hopeful.

"That's not how it—I mean, *is* that how that song goes? It sounded a bit off."

"Oh, yeah. I was just being silly. I haven't played this old thing in forever, but I think it still has a few songs left in it."

"You should keep working on it. I really like it." It was absolutely true. The lyrics might not match, the bass and the voice might waver from lack of practice, and the pacing might need work, but Megan loved seeing her mother like this.

"Thank you, honey. You want to show me what you've been learning in those voice lessons?"

Megan paused, a little unsure how to respond, since the voice lessons had been a bit of a sore topic at times, but she realized that, yes, even as tired as she was, singing to her mother's playing was precisely what she wanted. "Yeah, but you're going to need to play something I know."

Megan's mother nodded, putting her fingers back to the strings, before pausing, looking thoughtful, as if trying to figure out something she knew that Megan would as well. Finally, with a small nod as she settled on something, she looked to Megan. "I'm pretty sure this has been on the radio when we were both in the car," she said, before starting to play.

Megan didn't need the rest of the guitars or the beat, quickly picking up on Better Than Ezra's most famous bassline. The lyrics weren't overly complicated, and while her mother was still imperfect in places, it was easily close enough. She launched into the song about better times, and living in those times with someone who was no longer there. Despite the subject, the song was catchy, and oddly hopeful, which, considering her mother playing, her fingers recalling old times, and her life back then, seemed somehow perfect.

As she hit the middle of the song, her mother had stopped wavering and missing notes, the playing, while quiet, in perfect time. Not having to divide her attention between singing and playing probably helped, but Megan liked to think a lot of it was simply coming back to her as she got into the song and just let herself play.

The song ended all too soon, and with it, some of the exhaustion that had been temporarily suspended as she got into the music hit Megan again, and she moved to lean against the back of a chair, catching her breath just a little, though she couldn't have stopped smiling had she wanted to.

"Megan, that was really, really good. I'm impressed."

Megan blinked in surprise, then blushed. "Thanks. It runs in the family, though. Cassia said you were really, really good, you know, back when you played. I think you still are."

"Cassia, Cassia... she's Lani's friend who busks down by the stadium, and plays some shows up in Fremont, right?"

"Yeah, in Fremont and at a bunch of other local clubs and stuff. They'll be playing at the Fair tomorrow. You should come see them with us." She quickly inhaled and held her breath, realizing what she'd said. Her mother might work in the industry still, for most of the bigger music venues, but she never actually went to shows.

Sheila O'Reilly paused, drumming her fingers on the bass. Megan could only imagine that much the same thoughts were occurring to her mother.

Finally, after what was probably several seconds, but seemed far longer to Megan, her mother responded. "Are you sure you want your mom along for that? You're sixteen, aren't you supposed to think I'll embarrass you?" She was smiling, but Megan could see hints of genuine worry in her mother's eyes, as if she was not at all sure about interacting with her daughter on this type of level.

"What? My mom the former rock-star? I wish I could be that cool."

Sheila laughed, one brief laugh, caught off guard. "My rock star days are behind me, honey. But if that's really okay with you, I'd love to come and see your friend play."

Megan sighed with relief, and moved to the couch to hug her mother, leaning across one side of the bass a little. "Thanks, Mom. I'd love to talk more, or try another song, but we, uhm, really walked a lot today. And, uhm, helped carry a lot of stuff around. I should probably get some sleep." Whatever adrenaline she'd had on walking in to see her mother playing had faded with the end of the song, and she was feeling the effects of the long day again.

"Oh, okay. Sure thing, honey. I'm going to try that song a couple more times. I think I can do better. Then I'll head for bed. I don't want to keep you up."

Megan smiled wider and shook her head. "Practice as long as you want. I'll sleep just fine. I guarantee it."

Megan managed to hit the bathroom to brush her teeth and clean up before bed—and was startled to see herself in the mirror. How had her mother not noticed? Her hair was a mess, her hands and arms bore scrapes and a couple shallow cuts, her clothes were muddy, and any kind of close inspection revealed a couple of bloodstains as well.

Hearing her mother's voice in her head, she did her best to pre-treat the worst stains with water and a bit of soap to try to salvage the outfit, and then managed her way through brushing her hair a little, then brushing her teeth, by rote. By the time she was done, she was staggering to her room. Though she'd had every intention when she left the bathroom of changing for bed, she ended up falling fast asleep within seconds of sitting down on the bed to take her shoes off.

Chapter 19: Rushed and Real

Megan woke with a start to her mother's voice. "Megan, get ready. Breakfast in fifteen minutes!" She started to get up, then dropped back to her pillow with a groan. Everything hurt, most especially her feet. A little more time was spent debating how long she could stay in bed and still get downstairs in time.

Then she thought of her reflection in the mirror, the mud, the bloodstains, the scrapes and the messy, tangled hair. She decided a hot shower might be the best option for aching muscles and making sure that her mother didn't ask too many awkward questions. Rediscovering the bass the previous night might have distracted her from thinking too much about Megan's appearance, but it couldn't last forever.

The water was almost scalding, but it did ease some of the sore muscles. She bandaged her scrapes as subtly as she could, then had to spend longer than she wanted trying to get her hair untangled and brushed out. Her mother was calling her down for breakfast, and then saying she was 5 minutes late and it was getting cold, by the time she finished pulling on a new shirt and jeans. She tried to dash towards the dining room to show she was hurrying, before it turned into a bit of a quick limp instead.

It was only when she saw the layout that she paused to consider the oddity of her mother cooking breakfast. The O'Reillys certainly recognized 'the most important meal of the day,' but it was usually a meal of boring cereals, milk, and fruit, served with vitamins. There were exceptions, but they usually didn't involve pancakes, scrambled eggs, ham, and makeshift hashbrowns.

"What's the occasion?" she asked as she sat down, wincing and wishing she'd been more careful with her words, as if this new take on her mother could break at any moment, and the woman she'd left before the fair could return if she said or did anything wrong.

"Going to my first concert in..." she paused, trying to count the years, "Going to a concert with my daughter. I thought something a little special was in order. And you'll need your energy.

I looked up Sax & Violins on the internet last night. Apparently it's a very high energy show."

Of course she'd looked them up. Megan also noted bits of green amidst the eggs, which turned out, on closer examination, to be spinach, and diced apples in the pancakes. When the glass of milk was added, the breakfast might be unusually extravagant, but it was still balanced—despite the changes, this Sheila O'Reilly was still definitely her mother, and somehow that made Megan feel a lot better. The two sides of her had apparently coexisted well enough, as the obsessively organized album liner notes and extra band supplies in storage had attested.

"Yeah," Megan finally said. "This is going to be fun." She was sure of it. And once breakfast was done, she went back upstairs and took her medication, saving half of the multi-colored pills for later.

"I think that's Lani's car pulling up outside," her mother called eventually. "I'll meet you for the concert at 5."

"Thanks, Mom." Megan hobbled back down the stairs and straight for the front door. "Yeah, that's *Space Ship!* So I'll see you then."

Justin, in his full Seahawks livery, was already stepping out to get Megan's door. Seeing him and Lani—who looked every bit as worn as Megan felt, and with even more scrapes and bruises evident—brought her mind back to the situation.

"So... what do we do until the concert?" she asked as she sat down.

"Take in the Fremont Fair," Lani said.

"Right." After all the excitement yesterday, it seemed like there should be something more, or something big and obvious happening. The dead didn't rise from their graves every day, after all, at least as far as she knew. Likewise, Ashling apparently hadn't seen her former captor in years, and suddenly he just turned up.

She tried to settle her racing thoughts by assuring herself that they'd foiled the Butterfly Collector's attempts to collect all the shrouds... for whatever reason he wanted them. Her thoughts quickly responded back that he still had half the map, and maybe he only needed one or two of them, or that he might try and send the other wights for the ones he hadn't collected.

As Megan stared out the window, pondering this and keeping an eye out for the Center of the Universe, she heard the edge of conversation—and as she slowly realized what it was, she was all the more determined to keep her eyes out the window.

"You're not married, are you, Justin?" Lani asked.

"No, my family were landed and respectable, but I wasn't the heir to a dukedom or anything that would require marrying young. I certainly wasn't even going to start thinking of that sort of stuff until I'd earned my knighthood."

"Well, you earned your knighthood a few years early, as it happens. Granted, a few centuries late chronologically, but a few years early in your life."

"Yes, well, with all due respect to him, his Majesty cheated some there."

Getting to the fair was a welcome relief. By the time they found parking, they had a walk of several blocks, but the spectacle was already coming to them. Flags flew everywhere, with even more rainbows than usual for Fremont. Jugglers filled the air with asymmetrically rhythmic color, and buskers filled it with music.

People thronged the sidewalks, thousands upon thousands of very human people. Megan briefly found herself walking near a green woman. She wasn't about to mistake her for a jade statue, though. The body paint had none of the eerie perfection of some Faerie complexions. With all that had been going on, part of her found something very comforting about that.

There were also numerous pauses as they moved, so Megan, Justin, or often both could say hello to some of the many dogs being taken down to the fair, once they verified with the various owners that it was all right to do so. Megan spared a moment to hope Cassia'd have no problem carrying the basket of kittens from her home to the stage, but with so much adorable fur needing scritches, a moment was all she could spare.

Once they reached the various canopy tents lining the street, bedecked with streamers and bead curtains, they spent a while window shopping. Lani picked up some rosehip-scented liniment at an apothecary, applying it to one wrist and elbow before offering it to Megan. "This is good stuff. Better than aspirin. You should try it." she suggested, gesturing back to the middle-aged woman in the booth. "She does good work."

"What did you pay for it with?" Megan asked as she reached for the bottle.

"Cash," Lani said with a sigh. "But asking is a good sign, even if in the wrong place."

They skipped buying anything else, but Megan spent a lot of time examining the various arts and crafts, which were in abundance at the fair, while Lani had to stop every time they passed a booth selling books. Eventually, tired feet and sore muscles won out, and they bought drinks and went to sit on the grass for a while, listening to the music coming from a rooftop party across the street from the fair.

Parts of the crowd were just starting to drift towards the parade route when Lani insisted they'd done enough resting, and should go find a good spot to watch the parade from.

"My feet still hurt. Five more minutes?" Megan asked.

"You at least have a hope of seeing over someone if we don't get right in front. I don't want to spend another year hearing about it second hand later. Let's go."

And soon there were marching bands, their different songs blending and un-blending with the rooftop parties and everything else. There were dancing troupes and hula hoops. There were many, many packs of bicyclists, some of them even fully clothed. Either way, the colors were bright.

"Lani?" Megan asked quietly—as quietly as the ruckus from the interweaving musics would allow.

"What?"

"How much of … all this... is... People Like Us? And like Cassia?"

Lani sighed. "Megan, yes: a lot of the community of … Folk are going to come to something like this. So will 59,900 other people. We're not the predominant force. People Like Us play an important role, but the whole revelry and creative spark can still be 99% human.

"Yeah, I guess it can." And Megan smiled and looked forward to her mother's arrival.

Chapter 20: Sax & Violins

"Megan, honey, can you draw Mack another maze? He solved the last one you did. Well, eventually. He kept running into your minotaur on purpose over and over."

Megan nodded to Mrs. Kahale's request cheerfully and set into making a new maze while Mrs. Kahale explained the rules for the concert, though the list was fairly short, since Megan's mother was going to be there. The teens nodded their understanding, or the girls did, while Justin solemnly swore his. He verified he'd keep an eye on the girls, since they were more prone to getting lost or pinned in by the crowd.

As she, Lani, and Justin started to mill through people towards the stage, Megan could manage to hear Mack navigating his LEGO figure through the maze, this time complete with a LEGO dragon on his treasure horde.

"What's that about?" She caught her mother asking. "Keeps him busy, obviously, but..."

"Megan draws them for him whenever I'm trying to tell the girls something important," Mrs. Kahale answered, sighing as Mack voiced his LEGO man's death scene when he ran into the dragon the first time.

"Oh, I'm sorry she wasn't paying attention."

"Oh, she was. That's why I give her the paper, so she'll draw instead of daydream."

"...Oh. That's...that's good. Really good."

Megan focused on keeping up with Lani and Justin.

They got up to the stage early, despite the protests of Megan's feet. Somehow, resting and having an early dinner of fair food out on the grass from the end of the parade to the start of the concert didn't do a lot to ease the pain, but for this, she managed. Megan's mother, not having to deal with aching muscles and swollen feet, caught up not long after. They reached the barricade, but only barely, as the concert area filled up quickly, leaving only a little room to move.

The crowd quieted as the first violin notes echoed out from one edge of the stage, then went silent. A moment later, it was answered by a violin with a slightly deeper tone, playing from the other edge. At first, the sounds were classical, almost precisely what one might expect when attending a show featuring violins, save the fact they were obviously electric and amped. After four back-and-forths, with increasingly complex progressions, the violins sped up, still playing the classical melody, but at a much more rapid pace.

Three more musical duels of challenge and answer, and the music shifted entirely, as the two violinists finally came on stage, battling it out with familiar rock chords. The two players closed in on one another, moving to the time of their music, one approaching as the other stilled, until they were up close and glaring at one another, sawing on their bows.

Another figure, smaller than either, wearing green robes, stepped between them. Until she shoved the violinists apart, Megan hadn't seen her, but supposed that had the most to do with the dueling pair making a spectacle of themselves.

Her attention was pulled away again, as Cassia played a wail on her saxophone. Megan quickly realized that the band had taken their spots on stage while the violinists played—the pair who were now stepping backwards to the beat of an emerging drumbeat, not taking their eyes off of one another.

Finally, Nell threw off the green robes, revealing jeans and a band t-shirt beneath. Cassia's saxophone wail trailed off. The drums stopped, and as the beat ended, the violinists froze in place, fixed, unblinking, glaring across the stage at one another.

Nell grabbed the microphone, but let the silence reign for several more seconds. Then she began to sing. Her voice carried, far more than Megan had expected from such a small woman. Even as the other instruments kicked back in, she had no trouble being heard, and her words understood, above them. The sounds of the band's "Soft Drink Conspiracy" rose and fell. YouTube hadn't done it justice. Nell sang high and low, displaying a startling range. Throughout it all, she stood almost stock still at the mic stand, closing her eyes, and just letting her voice sweep out over the crowd like an incoming tide.

Though Nell might have become the visual focal point as she started singing, the original spotlight stealers quickly took visual attention back. The two violins circled her, circled Cassia, and moved about the stage. Aside from the occasional theatrical spin, they never took their eyes off of each other, and from the expressions and motions, Megan swore that at any moment, they might forget the violins and start swordfighting with one another with the bows. As often as not, they mirrored each other, advancing and retreating, stalking and circling, playing all the while with a feverish intensity.

Cassia was much more stationary—instead of stalking and dancing about the stage, her sheer presence and skill with the sax dragged the imaginary spotlight to her at times. Perhaps it was the contrast between her muscular bulk and the tiny singer, or just Cassia's personality, but she almost loomed, and the sax alternately blasted or wailed its notes.

It took Megan a few moments to notice that the violinists' footfalls were not just rhythmic, but were still perfectly timed to the drumbeats, picking up and slowing down as if the drums might be the echo of footfalls about the stage, timed with the song, even matching the occasional furious assault on the drums.

And the bass... well, Megan had to admit Erin was good. Possibly very good. She hit all the notes. She kept up with the band. It still seemed a little bit to Megan like watching the band teacher jamming with a bunch of seasoned pro rockers. Nothing was actually out of place, but she was just playing, occasionally looking at her bass, occasionally watching the show the others put on. The more Megan watched, the more she realized that Sax & Violins were playing a set, sure, but more than that, this was theater.

The band finished the first song, letting the last notes of Nell's voice intertwine with the fading echo of the saxophone. The drums paused, and, with the beat, the violinists froze again. The crowd stilled once more, with Megan glad for the brief respite from the crush of bodies.

Seeing the smaller girls hemmed in, Justin extended his arms, taking firm hold of the barricade to Megan's right and Lani's left, and dug himself in to protect them more. The barricade guard at first moved towards him, then saw the intent, and just nodded, stepping back into position.

Megan spared a glance for her mother, to make sure she was taking it all well. Sheila O'Reilly was looking almost mesmerized, eyes locked on the stage, but otherwise seemed just fine.

After the few seconds of rest, the violins took the place of guitars, and Nell joined them in launching into Neil Young's "Cinnamon Girl." Megan had heard the song a number of times before, but never with quite so much frantic intensity. The classic song got more of the aging Seattle hippies and new agers into the set, while the band's punk rock take ignited those who'd already been dancing hard to the first song in the list.

They followed up by slowing down the pace, but upping the power, Nell's voice blasting out dark lyrics that blended failed relationships, pessimism, and poetry to a background of bass and drums and accompaniment of a crying saxophone. Megan didn't know the song, but recognized some of the lyrics as being borrowed from old poems she'd covered in English class, blended with punk rock lyricism. The end effect was sort of like beat poetry on steroids. It wasn't as danceable as the first songs, but had just as much power — and as much effect on the crowd.

Nell finally trailed off, and the rest of the band followed, one instrument after another. Far more cheerfully than the song would suggest, Nell followed by talking to the crowd.

"And that was 'Never Read Robert Frost After You've Just Stabbed Someone's Black Heart.' In the spirit of not ending on an anti-climax, we've got an impulse for something special. It has come to our attention that a legend is present tonight. Could Ms. Sheila O'Reilly please consider coming to join us?"

There was a buzz through the crowd, with some excited voices, while others tried to figure out who that was without saying anything, lest other, more knowledgeable music fans find out they had no idea who Sheila O'Reilly was or why the band called her a legend.

Sheila was frozen with indecision, mouth open, like she was about to say something, but no sound was coming out. Finally, Megan's mother, dressed in her most casual clothes, which a lot of people could still have gotten away with wearing to the office, looked at her daughter, to find her bouncing and cheering.

"Go, go!" Megan shouted, waving towards the stage.

As soon as Sheila made the motion to start climbing the barricade, Cassia pointed her out to security, who let her pass, and escorted her onto the stage.

Erin, all smiles, gave up her bass in return for a chance to hug Sheila O'Reilly, to huge cheers, and then stepped back to take a mic as a backup singer, while Sheila tested out the unfamiliar instrument. The band had apparently adapted the Late for the Party song Megan had asked for the day before, or—given Cassia, Violet, and Erin's appreciation for Sheila's basswork—it was possible they'd already done so. Regardless, "Yet Another Song About Jumping" was well suited to Sax & Violins. Despite their punk roots, they dove right in to the high energy, poppy, danceable song, giving it their own spin, with the violinists putting on their own rapid, leaping dance on stage, playing all the while. Nell took the lead, belting out the lyrics, letting Sheila focus on her basswork first and foremost.

"Well you're the hottest person / I could ever hope to meet.
But if we tried to tango, / I'd be stepping on your feet."

Megan watched her mother as the song progressed. Sheila stared at her hands a little at first, then looked up to take in the rest of the stage as her hands continued the infectiously bouncy foundation of the lightly satirical music.

"So let's be life-affirming/ —or is that too big a word?
Let's see how popular it/ gets to 'not follow the herd.'"

By the time they got to the chorus, Sheila had gotten used to the familiar old bassline, and was more than ready to join Erin in adding backing vocals and urging the crowd to dance, and those who remembered the 15-year-old song to sing along the first time through.

"Now I want you to dance, / Now I want you to sing."

"You can get the lyrics wrong / They don't mean a thing."

By the time they hit the third and final chorus, everyone in the audience was chanting along.

Sheila played two more songs with the band, a Breeders cover and one more Late for the Party song. Then she made her way back to the girls and to a huge hug from Megan. Sheila O'Reilly looked exhausted, with hair mussed enough to show up Megan's unruly red locks, her blouse was untucked, she was sweating and out of breath—but outside of some of Megan's baby pictures, she didn't think she'd ever seen her mother smile like that.

When the set was finished, Megan, Justin, Lani, and Sheila were allowed backstage. Erin almost immediately set on Sheila to get some pointers and a new autograph, while the teens stepped aside with Cassia.

"Cass, that was amazing!" Megan immediately said.

"Oh, that was just the warm-up," she said with a big, toothy, Cassia grin. "Now it's time for the *real* show."

Chapter 21: Best Seats in the House

"Just another hour?" her mother asked again.

"Just another hour," Megan assured.

Sheila O'Reilly looked at Cassia. "No alcohol or other drugs, and no ... well, no more naked people than Fremont-standard?"

"Not for this next hour," Cassia assured.

"Okay, that's relatively believable ... have we ever actually met, Cassia?"

"I couldn't say," the satyress who'd been in the Seattle music scene for decades replied with a shrug.

Sheila looked back to Megan. "Lani'll bring you home?"

"Yep." Megan wasn't sure if she'd felt this nervous between wight expeditions.

Finally, her mother smiled. "Okay. Always good to properly celebrate a record-setting GPA. I'm going to go home and collapse, but I'm going to leave the alarm clock in the hallway set for an hour, okay?"

"Okay. Thanks, Mom!"

The small group set to helping the band, Finn, and the rest of the stage crew in carrying the band's things, before the troll turned his attention to distributing new passes. "Yer all set. Have fun!" he called, returning to playing very imposing bouncer at the door while everyone disappeared back into Faerie, and the Goblin Market, one by one.

As much as she was tempted to go through and watch a couple of the performers, or walk down the long stretch of artists one more time, Megan let Lani lead her directly towards the stage. Her father sat on a raised dais in an ornate chair, with the Count on one arm and Ashling on the other exchanging eye-rolls with some of the attending sprites.

The Seelie Queen, with all her alien regality, had her own ornate chair not far away. It took Megan a moment to realize what was out of place there: General Inwar, usually a fixture at Orlaith's side every time she'd seen the Queen, was missing.

Megan settled in next to her father, sitting on the railing of the dais for the time being, to get off her feet. Lani joined her, but Justin, now in full knightly duty mode, stood sentry behind them. The band set up on the ornate stage, which was simultaneously a lot bigger and fancier than the one they had in Fremont, and, to Megan's eyes, so classical in design that it seemed a very odd place for a punk rock band to be setting up. On the other hand, she had to suppose that that was part of the entertainment value to the band themselves.

Megan managed to say a few words to her father, but nothing of consequence, as he was still being regularly distracted by messages from various sprites, and other members of his court. Just as that seemed to be settling down, Inwar entered, moving quickly, flanked by two knights. The General reached the Queen's side, leaned in to whisper something to her—whatever it was was met with a grave nod, but no words from Orlaith—then Inwar took his usual place to the right of her chair. All the while, stage hands of various species dragged what appeared to be white, grey, and black stone debris out onto the stage. Megan wasn't sure precisely why, but assumed that either the band had a use for it, or that it was some faerie thing she wouldn't understand.

The music started much as it had before, with the dueling violins. Now, however, they had even more space to use in their dance/duel, and all of the debris, bits of stone steps, collapsed slabs, broken columns, and the rest let them climb, leap, and even hide from one another before making dramatic leaps, in their athletic duel around the stage.

Nell came in right after the violins. Megan wasn't entirely sure if it was the acoustics of the place, or entirely her voice being really let loose, or some combination, but the woman went from just having a startling range to downright unearthly, as she sang the lyrics to a song Megan had heard from her internet research, but never quite like this, as Nell belted out the lyrics to "Elephants All the Way Down."

Once they were applauding, Megan muttered to her father. "They say she doesn't like to get involved with people like us—or herself—that much." She didn't ask the question.

Riocard smiled. "Well, when the family business involves drowning sailors or crushing them against rocks... some people like the refreshing quality of a quiet life by different waters."

"Oh. Yeah. I'd guess so."

As popular as the opening number was, the court—and probably the rest of the market, though Megan's view was limited—really erupted into frenzied dancing and singing when the second song of the set began. Cassia wailed away on the saxophone, and the violins alternated between light, airy major keys and simple notes, all to a steady beat, as Nell sang the start of each verse, sing-songing the words to nursery rhymes. Then each one took a dark turn, with minor keys, erratic beats, and twisted subtexts. A few of the lyrics to "Four and Twenty Blackbirds" left Megan feeling a little bit twitchy, especially recalling old memories of her mother singing them to her long ago, but throughout the song, of those on the dais, Ashling and—particularly—the Count were dancing and bouncing as if it was the greatest song ever.

Then it all stopped, the lights to the stage abruptly shut off, with just one violin—probably Violet's, Megan figured—playing the strains of the simple sixpence-melody until it faded completely. Applause and cheers filled the vacuum of silence for a few moments, but the silence outlived it, the stage still shrouded in darkness.

Then the steady pulse of the bass started. Then Nell began to sing quietly, so very quietly, as one stage light was allowed to blink along.

These past two years (and one was leap), / I've found it hard to get to sleep. / Fluorescent lights pulse, / Match the beat of our skulls / and make sterile shadows look steep.

Another Late to the Party cover. Nell was, it was soon revealed, singing with herself, but "Psych Ward Composition" had originally been a duet between Megan's parents. It was a high-energy creepy descent into madness, but it had been recorded in the days when they were posing for smiling pictures with newborn Megan. It was strange to be hearing Cassia's girlfriend take her violin into the erratic notes while Megan sat beside her father.

The band took a break between the third and fourth songs, with Nell talking to the crowd. After the numerous twists and turns of the songs, the visual display, and the memories involved, Megan found herself just staring.

"Silver dollar for your thoughts?" her father asked. At her expression, he laughed in that dark-chocolate way she'd come to expect. He handed her an actual coin, dated 1904. "I don't carry pennies, after all."

Megan nodded toward the stage. "Cassia brought her here. She tells her about places like this—and about being a satyr."

"Yes. She does. And one day, it will be over—perhaps next month, perhaps in twenty-five years, when Miss Baptiste's hands can no longer hold a bow. Either way, it's going to be difficult for Miss Baptiste to come away from it all, knowing what she knows, and the former is far more likely than the latter."

"Mr. and Mrs. K have been together for nineteen years."

"The kahuna is very clever. He is also very lucky."

"...The what? I thought he was a menehune."

"He is. Kahuna is a job description, as a master of traditional craftsmanship."

"Okay. So he's smart. So're...a lot of people." Megan barely managed not to say 'you.'

Riocard nodded. "But not everyone is smart in the same ways. The kahuna... understands a great deal about building things to last. And he pours a great deal of himself into maintaining what he's built. And when it ends, well, the kahuna will have a very hard time coming away from it, knowing what he knows."

Megan paused, thinking about that. She'd seen Mr. Kahale with his family. Then she considered just how long her father had lived, or even Cassia, and maybe Ashling, depending on which Ashling story was to be believed. She didn't miss the connection to the talk of Cassia's girlfriend, either. Apparently, too much contact between mortals and the faeries wasn't only potentially hard on the mortals. She didn't like the implications, but thought, perhaps, she understood her father a little better.

She was still pondering that one as Cassia stepped up to a mic to alternate playing the sax and providing added vocals on the next song. This one didn't involve so much athleticism, and wasn't as danceable, but was just as distracting as Megan tried to follow the lyrics. She'd heard this one as well, plainly and accurately titled "The One With the Complicated Rhyme Scheme." The live performance did better highlight the weird chord progressions, echoing vocals, and backing vocals that actively contrasted the lead singer's lyrics. Through it all, the clever wordplay explored the conventions of poetry like particularly sadistic English professors.

Megan looked to Justin. She certainly hadn't asked him to be her date, and he certainly wasn't acting like one, standing like that when there was already plenty of other security around. Of course, all things considered, she couldn't blame him for wanting to be professional. Court stuff was tricky enough without at-large collectors of butterflies and the undead.

The band immediately followed up with *Beethoven's Third*, with more saxophone, and occasional interruptions for some reason Megan didn't understand, with Nell complaining about Napoleon in at least three languages. Once she thought about it, what did make complete sense to Megan, though, was the crowd rocking out to Beethoven as readily as they had to contemporary punk.

Naturally, the band immediately followed Beethoven with a cover of "Radioactive." After the two song break, she supposed for the good of the violinists, the two were right back in fine form, fencing and stalking one another about the stage while they played.

When the song ended, the band took another short break, with Nell talking to the audience and the band collecting some water, the drummer, Erin, and Cassia drinking, both violinists going directly to just pouring it over themselves as soon as the instruments were securely put aside.

Meanwhile, on the dais, another messenger arrived. This sprite, moth wings flapping frantically, careened towards General Inwar, almost crashing to a stop. Ashling and the sprite exchanged a glare, while Megan got a better look at the messenger, dressed in an odd hodgepodge of tiny furs and scraps of denim. She knew this one: Gilroy was one of Peadar's gang. Gilroy and Ashling had, for lack of a better term, bad blood. He perhaps meant to whisper the message, but in his state, Megan, and others nearby, couldn't help but overhear.

"There's a crack in the ice."

That was when the trouble started.

Chapter 22: The Crowd Goes Wild

The first reactions were from the others on the dais. The Queen's guards, both those already on watch, and those who'd come in flanking Inwar, moved immediately to guard positions. Riocard's men, more than Megan had realized had been hanging about, drew their weapons. Justin looked as if he might follow suit, but instead simply shifted position, hand on the hilt of the sword.

Word rippled rapidly down through the crowd, and the muttering grew to shouting—and shoving, and growling. Some people pressed towards the stage to make demands, but the guardsman were already in position to still any nascent rioting.

Megan looked to the stage, where Cassia appeared ready to play one-girl army if anyone from the agitated crowd tried to climb up.

"Good night, Everybody!" Nell announced as she quickly ushered the band off the stage with most of their equipment.

Even the queen looked startled, her dawn-colored eyes widening and her inhumanly delicate long fingers gripping the arms of her chair tightly as she looked towards Inwar.

Indeed, there were only two signs of absolute calm amidst the chaos. General Inwar was one of them, directing the guards, calling out commands in a voice that rang over the noise, rallying Sidhe knights and others to form up near the dais at his call for order. Once the first lines were formed, others under his command started to seed themselves throughout the room, to be in position for whatever might come.

The other was Riocard, who lounged in his chair, regarding the riot like it might be a planned part of the entertainment. He called for no one and directed nothing, only bothering to briefly make sure that his daughter stayed properly within the secured area for now.

Despite the chaos that had begun, those Unseelie nearest Riocard looked to him, initially unsure, and many calmed, making their way in the crowd. A few knotted together into gangs, while others sauntered towards the doors in an I-do-as-I-will fashion.

Others among the Unseelie, of course, continued to push and shove, or make demands, as did a smaller, but still notable portion of the Seelie, ignoring calls for order. Being faeries, Megan noted, some few of the audience who had been mostly in order only started shoving and shouting when doing so specifically defied attempts to restore order as well, but, for the moment, that was a minority.

Gilroy looked oddly exhausted for a faerie, while also looking reasonably pleased with the ruckus, making Megan wonder just how accidental his stage whispering had been.

"Does this have something to do with Balor's officers and stuff?" Megan asked her father.

"Balor?" As she echoed the name questioningly, the Seelie Queen no longer looked merely startled. She attempted to look at Riocard with her usual intense expression, but her head tilted at a strange, nervous angle.

"Ah. Do excuse me, Majesty," Riocard said sedately. "I must not have sent you the memo."

"What does … *he* … have to do with a problem at the sealed lake?" Orlaith asked.

"I have no idea, or even if he does. There's just been some minor trouble about some of his hangers-on and souvenirs recently."

Megan tried not be too blatant about her annoyance at hearing it called 'minor trouble.' She knew Lani was doing the same. Justin never seemed to struggle, his face professionally blank. She often wondered just how bad 14th-Century politics were, that he could get that good a poker face at his age.

Inwar was giving orders in a language Megan didn't understand, but his lieutenants clearly did, leaving one by one to relay the messages to their own troops. Inwar moved a hand to the Queen's shoulder, and her expression calmed somewhat as he continued to focus on sending his people out to handle things for him beyond the concert hall. As soon as he'd sent out everyone he dared risk while the concert hall was still on the verge of chaos, he leaned in, speaking quietly to the Queen, while she answered in the same hushed tones.

Finally, another messenger sprite flew over the not-quite-panicked crowd. This one reported to Riocard. "Some people to see you, Majesty. The dullahan and some others."

The Unseelie King nodded and stood up on the dais, gesturing for Megan to do the same. He indicated the sprite could go back about his business, then turned to Ashling. "Can you go guide the dullahan and his crew to the little blue tent across the way? I think we'll meet them for tea." Ashling nodded her understanding, then climbed on the crow's back. They took off to bear the information and directions, while Riocard simply stepped down the stairs of the dais. "Megan, Miss Kahale, Sir Justin, you're with me."

The Seelie crowd control and partial evacuation was continuing. Riocard spared no glance for them. Some of the Unseelie were still agitating. They nevertheless stepped aside as Riocard walked calmly into the crowd, the way simply parting before him. Megan and Lani followed much less casually, hurrying to stay close. The girls looked back to see Justin following closely behind them, his hand still on the hilt of the sword. Behind him on the dais, Orlaith was staring, quite possibly at the back of Megan's father's head, as he didn't turn to look at all.

Riocard led Megan and her friends to the quiet little blue tent, which somehow seemed to contain an entire Japanese tea-house on the inside, wooden structures, carvings, and all, despite the humble appearance outside the flap of the tent.

As soon as they'd been seated, kneeling around a low table with tea, with the chaos sounding very far away, Megan finally confronted her father, now that she was certain they were away from the Queen and her entourage, and the other Unseelie hadn't arrived yet. "Aren't you going to, you know, do something?" She managed to avoid yelling, but only barely. Even when it wasn't his season, her father had to finally realize something was serious, right?

Riocard paused, glancing at his daughter with a smile. "I already have. Inwar and the Queen have order. Their people need commands. They need regimentation. They'll listen, as long as someone appears to take charge. I have monsters. They don't like orders. They don't like to feel constraints. They don't want to hear about what's necessary."

"But it is necessary."

"It's all about the phrasing, dearest."

An odd-looking crew entered the house, including a few sprites that Megan didn't recognize, the figure with the rabbit ears, two leprechauns, three redcaps, a snaggle-toothed troll, and then the man in black with the removable head. The sprites took places atop the table. The others, after a brief pause, knelt at places around the table, some looking very much out of place in the quiet surroundings, and some looking uncomfortable doing so, but none argued with the choice of venue or Riocard's example of following the establishment's customs.

The headless man, dressed in colonial-style black clothing, complete with a cravat that met empty air at the neck—the dullahan, Megan supposed—took the most prominent position among the newcomers, directly across from Riocard

"So when the note got passed around yesterday," a voice began, from under the man's arm, where the head was tucked with a grin that would fit in with the redcaps. "We got to thinking about those officers."

Then the dullahan whipped off his 'cape', folding over his arm what Megan now recognized as another shroud. Then he removed a bag from his waist, opening it, and removing a severed head from the bag—a head, Megan realized, with the same nearly skeletal thinness and empty eyes of the wights they'd fought, once they were rendered dead a second time.

"My grandad fought against one, used to take us on family picnics 'round this time of year to the tomb."

"You'd have family picnics at the booby-trapped grave of someone who'd tried to kill him?" Megan asked, before covering her mouth, looking to her father to see if she'd spoken out of turn.

The dullahan shifted his own head into his hand enough to show her that his eyebrow was raised. "Yeah. How does your family do festive? Anyway, the wight was a bit holed up in the place—

behind barricades, working on fixing his siege engines—but you know how my horse and I are about making our way past gates."

The dullahan briefly juggled the two heads and the shroud with a performer's flourish. "So if there's some kind of wight scavenger hunt," he said as the cloth and the wight's head landed right in front of Riocard. "We're in."

Megan couldn't help staring. "Whoa," she said.

"Indeed," her father's rich, dark voice concurred. "Two asymmetric spheres and a cloth are always harder to juggle than three objects of a kind. Well done, sir."

When the Unseelie crew left, Riocard smiled at Megan again. "We don't want to hear about necessary. But if we hear we're being hedged out, or out-monstered, we certainly won't stand for it."

Megan considered that, as her father re-wrapped the head, keeping it, before folding the shroud and offering it to Megan. "So, you just put word out, act like it's no big deal, and someone goes wight hunting. Nice," she said. "So, what now?"

"Now, someone said the B-word around Orlaith. She'll have more questions for me, and as it's her season, I'll answer them. It would be best if you were in Seattle when that happened."

"Balor?" Megan tried.

"Orlaith remembers Balor every time she forgoes looking in the mirror."

Chapter 23: At Home

"Do you think they'll get the rest of the wights?" Megan asked as they drove away from Fremont.

"I doubt it," Justin answered. He was staring out the window with the sheathed sword in his lap, not willing to stop being on watch yet. "They won't all spend time getting their siege weapons together. The last two are likely out of their tombs by now."

"At this point," Lani said, "I think they're the least of our worries."

Megan raised an eyebrow. "Because ancient undead officers aren't a big deal?"

"Not what I mean. Sure, they're bad, but they're just one part of something."

"Okay, so we need to find the Butterfly Collector. I mean, if Dad's people don't find him first. They'll probably bring his head in next, right?"

"Won't that be nice, eh?" Ashling interjected with a smile that Megan knew should be disturbing her more. That it didn't was enough to make Megan worry about herself.

Lani sighed. "I don't think so. I think Ashling seeing him in the market is about as close as the fae are going to get on their own."

"What makes you say that? I mean, they've done okay for themselves a lot longer than we've been around, right? They have to have dealt with stuff like this before. Cassia even talks about the undead rising and stuff."

"Yeah, she does. And they probably have. But the Butterfly Collector has help on the inside."

"Robin Goodfellow, you mean?"

"Yeah, think about it," Lani said. "He's an expert in chaos, right?"

"Original Prankster," Ashling said. "Except without the part where 'pranks' imply harmless."

Lani nodded. "So the guy probably got some help and information. But that's not what's really bothering me."

"Let me guess, that would be your trigonometry homework for next year?"

Lani sighed. "Smartass. Okay, first, I already took trigonometry last year."

"Of course you did."

"I'm really looking forward to differential calculus."

"Of course you are."

"Second, and more importantly, it's not just that Robin Goodfellow is involved. Sure, that's bad. In fact, if a mortal has something that will get that kind of help, it's probably really big, but let's think smaller. If you have one of the world's most famous and apparently most powerful faeries on your side, and you have big plans to cause chaos, what do you do?"

"I hadn't really thought about it, why?"

"Because he has. He's thought this through, every step. If what he was doing was easy, the standard wouldn't have stayed there for so many centuries, and the wights would have gotten up before now. Yes, they've had undead incursions, but not these particular undead. It takes research and planning. I mean, how do you even get a hold of Robin Goodfellow, anyway? I've lived around this my whole life, and I certainly wouldn't know."

"Okay, so he's like you would be if you were a mad scientist or something."

"Mad engineer," Lani said.

"I'm sorry, what?"

"Most mad scientists aren't really scientists. They're not testing any theories. They're just building death rays. They're mad engineers."

"Okay, okay, so I stand corrected. Now, what were you saying before?"

"Okay, so he has Robin Goodfellow working for him, or with him, or something. And as soon as a wight gets away, Robin is right after us. Why?"

"Because he thought it would be fun?"

"On Robin's side, maybe. But with the market on, there must be a thousand fun things he could be doing. I think it was more intentional than that. We're wild cards. He thinks he has everything else planned, so he had to mess with us."

"You really think so?"

"There's plenty of people more powerful than us out there. Someone that careful isn't going to go mess with Balor's stuff if he doesn't have something to cover himself. He obviously knows how to get into Faerie, and he knows pixies and their ways of finding things." Lani looked vaguely apologetic as Ashling shuddered. "Maybe sprites too. If he couldn't counter those, they'd have found him already."

"Now I'm way more worried than I was. Why do you need to figure these things out in so much detail?"

Lani took one hand off the wheel, a rare gesture for her, to lean to the side and give Megan a one-armed hug. "Because, if I don't, you don't come up with brilliant plans to save the world."

When *Space Ship!* pulled into Megan's driveway, there was still plenty of time to disable the alarm clock in the hallway. Her mother seemed to have indeed gone straight to bed with a new kind of exhaustion. Megan urged Ashling to be quiet, and to just enter via her bedroom window, just in case, while Ashling urged Megan to remember her lessons about sneaking, before she climbed onto the Count, and they flew directly to Megan's room.

Megan found a snack, took her vitamins, and then got to her room without waking her mother. She sat down on her bed, managing to be too worried to fall asleep, despite physical exhaustion. "So, what now?"

"Now," said the pixie, cheerfully, "We make some music."

"Ashling, we can't wake my mom up," Megan hissed.

Ashling sighed. "First, your grammar is atrocious. Yes, we most certainly can wake your mother. It would be pretty easy. But we shouldn't. We have important work to do. Where is the music book?"

Megan dug around for a bit through her things to remember which hiding place she had it in, finally pulling out the book. "Right here, but I don't see how this is going to help. I can't go... I shouldn't go singing at this hour."

"Who said anything about singing? Well, except Aerosmith, Sesame Street, Bob Seger... the list goes on and on, but no matter what you've heard, you shouldn't be listening to Steven Tyler, except when you should. But not in this case."

Megan sighed. "Okay, okay, so not singing. Then what are we doing with the music book?"

Ashling smiled, wide-eyed, turning pages until she found one of the songs Megan had struggled with. "We're making music. Or rather, we're unmaking some music, so we can make others. Then, at some point, you can sing. But not right now."

Megan stared at the notes to the song, eyes homing in on the F-Sharps in particular. "Will that actually work?"

"I don't know. I've never unmade music before. Okay, okay, so there was one time, but I was drunk, and that tavern song was dangerously non-offensive. But no one remembers that song now, so it's okay. But I've never unmade music and expected it to work for a bard the new way. Nothing to do but give it a shot, though. Good thing you've got a lot of blank paper for recopying on."

While Ashling spoke, Megan was flipping through the music book. "Ooh! The storm-calling song hasn't got any F#s in it."

"That's good. The one you tried to use to save all our lives recently does, so break out the pen collection."

Megan worked with Ashling until she was too exhausted to keep her eyes open, worry or not. Between them, they retooled the counter-magic song, replacing parts of the melody that contained F#s with elements of other songs Ashling knew with similar effects. They planned tests to see if the songs would remain consistent without the original notes as written. Regardless, they weren't able to test the new composition while needing to be silent.

While it had felt like a lot at the time, when she woke up and double checked the music books and her extra paper, Megan found rather less progress, and a lot more doodling in the margins, than she'd remembered. Still, it was something.

Megan had breakfast with her mother, a much less ambitious effort than the day before, with her mother apologizing and citing a headache. Megan assured her that cereal was still perfectly good for breakfast most days and concernedly but chipperly recommended seeing a doctor if the headache went on.

She quietly hoped a reasonable doctor might take her mother off the extreme dosage of the green pills, if her moods had been steadily improving. When they were done with breakfast, including discussion of the concert, Sheila excused herself to get some work done, and Megan headed for the back yard to test the changes.

Ashling practiced moving small objects around, while Megan sang from the new songsheet to see if she could counteract the magic. There was no effect. Megan tried improvising. When this failed, Ashling tried a few suggestions as well. Whether she was basing them on long experience with bards and knowledge of the theories behind magic, or just trying to make Megan test her range with odd notes, sounds, and scales, Megan wasn't sure.

After what felt like a hundred failures, even if it was probably far fewer, Megan finally sat down to catch her breath, while trying to figure out what she was missing.

"Hey, don't look so depressed. We'll get it." Ashling offered, moving up to pat Megan's knee comfortingly.

"We will, but we're kind of in a hurry, and it would be good to maybe be able to do something more helpful."

"You were a lot of help. Think of all the things you did in those fights."

"Sure, but it took forever. Someone could have gotten a lot more hurt while I figured out the right song. And maybe I could have done something about that illusion."

"Maybe, maybe not. But remember what I said about trying too hard and faerie magic? If you keep trying to fret over every detail, the magic won't want to work with you. So, let's try this again. Breathe in, breathe out. Repeat as necessary."

Megan took a few deep breaths, reviewing the original song in her head. Every time she approached the troublesome notes, though, she lost the thread of thought, as if she couldn't even conceive of the sound of an F-sharp, much less sing it. "So, shouldn't it have gone really easily when I was all sleep-depped last night?

"Don't worry, you'll get it. But you need to relax and quit frowning so hard. My Cousin Nessa always had this technique for dark moods, see, she'd—"

Megan jumped up. "That's it!"

Now it was Ashling's turn to look confused. "Yes, it's really helpful, but first, I haven't even said it yet, and second, where are we going to get a horse-drawn carriage and a repeating crossbow?"

Megan blinked, mind going straight to thoughts of medieval drive-bys, before she got it back on track. "No, dark. Like, you know those songs we listened to on the internet, where they take a song, and change the key, and they sound all mournful and creepy, but awesome?"

Ashling nodded. "Not very danceable most of the time, though."

"Sure, but Faerie things do it all the time."

"Dance? Yeah, those are really popular."

"No, I mean that, say, when a guy is wearing a red cap, he could well be a healthy, normal American boy, even if it is '49ers gear. But if it's actually a magical cap dyed with blood, it takes on a *much darker tone.* Can we do that? Not the blood, the darker parallels. Like, keep the whole song, but put it in a completely different key to get rid of the sharps. Can you help?"

"Can I help drag a millennia-old, rousing Celtic ballad into the internet age and make the part where the prince rescues his true love sound like he's a creepy stalker? You bet!"

Chapter 24: Returning

Space Ship! was back in the driveway at lunchtime. Megan came out with a few pieces of paper in her back pocket. Ashling and the Count entered through one of the back passenger windows, while Megan said goodbye to her mother.

"Where are we eating?" Megan asked.

"At the Market, I hope," Lani said.

"Dad said he wanted us away for a bit," Megan said.

"He got his bit," Lani insisted. "Now I've got a hunch."

"Definitely not going to bet against your hunches. You okay with this, Justin?"

"Okay is a very complex term. I trust Lani, certainly."

They arrived at the Fremont Solstice Fair just in time for the dog parade. Lani wanted to get food, but agreed to pause on the side street while the various dogs, costumed and not, were led, or led their owners, through the streets. Megan, meanwhile, did her best to explain some of the costumes to Justin, who seemed more interested in these than he had the various body-painted people the day before. At least until she was reduced to an unintelligible squee as the dachshunds passed, two dressed in traditional Germanic festival dress, and the third, missing its back legs, with its mobility-assistance wheels and body partly encased in a little rolling beer keg.

Ashling and the Count conducted a few flyarounds, scouting out the sprawling fairgrounds, then eventually settled atop one of the canopy tents, once the teenagers picked out food after the parade. Cassia found them as they were finishing their lunch, the satyress joining them on the grass.

"Everyone okay?" Lani asked.

Cassia shook her head. "All of the band made it back safely. I'm giving all of them some space, since things back in Faerie are a mess. People found one more of the wight barrows, but the inhabitant was gone."

"And they haven't gotten the Huntsman and his hounds out after him?" Justin asked.

"Or a bunch of pixies, or, I guess, sprites might even be useful," Ashling added.

"That's just it," Cassia said, "They've done those things. Both courts have people looking. It's like the Butterfly Collector either doesn't exist, or we don't have enough information on him to give them a place to start, and the wights, well, something is protecting them."

Megan glanced at Lani, who was currently managing to look more irritated at the situation than she looked smug at being right about the level of preparation involved. "What could do that?" Megan asked.

"We saw some pretty powerful wards back on one of the wight barrows," Lani said, "The Fomoire had magic to rival the fae, and sometimes even the Gods. Maybe they're hiding out in one of the other burial mounds that wasn't on our map?"

Cassia nodded. "We have people in Ireland searching. Unfortunately, there's a lot of tombs out there. But we'll find them."

Megan said "We? But you're here. Looking after your girlfriend and the band and everything?"

Cassia shook her head. "Ric let me evacuate them, but asked me to do some scouting here, instead of joining the hunting parties in Faerie or Ireland."

"Scouting?" Justin asked, "What are they looking for here?"

"The Butterfly Collector had to have come from this side. He certainly didn't go through An Teach Deiridh. This is my stomping grounds, so Ric asked me to collect Ashling, and see if we can find any sign of him on this side. Knowing who he is might help. Or give the Huntsman a name."

"Just knowing his real name would help that much?" Megan asked.

"The Huntsman's magic is powerful, powerful stuff," Cassia said. "Ric doesn't think he had possession of the map for long enough, didn't use it enough, for it to count as his, or I'd be borrowing that. But yeah, a real name, and those hounds might be able to get past whatever protection he has hiding him."

"What about a receipt?" Megan asked.

"What are you talking about?" Justin said.

Megan glanced at Lani, who brightened, catching on to the idea quickly. "She's right," Lani said, "We don't know who he is, but we know where he's been shopping."

"We have to get back to the Goblin Market and find out where he bought the map." Megan said, getting up, with the others right after her.

"Are you sure that they can release that kind of information?" Lani said. "I mean, it seems like those kinds of shopping records are usually private, right?"

Justin said "They're still faeries. We have to convince them that it's in their best interests to tell us."

Ashling shook her head, letting Megan put the butterfly on her shoulder, while the Count took off and circled above. "That's not how it works. They have rules, but..."

"But," Megan said, "Even if they won't tell us just because, we can still get the information from them. The rule is that everything is for sale at the Goblin Market, right?"

"If you can pay for it," Ashling said, "Now you're catching on. I'm so proud of you."

They hurried to the stage as best they could through the people, moving around to the back to collect their passes. There, they found Finn sitting on the ground, laying back against the stage, eyes shut, snoring. One hand rested atop a red toy Volkswagen.

Robin Goodfellow was standing beside him with a smirk—and worse, with all of Finn's passes fanned out in front of him. "Now, now, you wouldn't be looking for these, would you?"

Justin's eyes didn't leave Robin, but he reached back and began to unzip the instrument case in which he was once more keeping the Sword of Light.

This was met with a countertenor giggle, which prompted Justin to pause in place. "Oh, yes," Robin said. "Please, yes. Pull out a weapon in the middle of 60,000 Seattleites. Doesn't matter if people can see the flames or not: the Sword is always a sword. You'll be waving it around in public, threatening a younger kid, 'cause I'm not staying put backstage if you try anything. At worst, you'll be stopped. At best—" there was another giggle and a toss of the long hair. "Panic in the crowds. We'll see if Fremont can manage a proper riot. Either way, when the police come, someone will end up looking into whatever visa you had 'arranged.' It may hold up normally, but not against assault charges. You'll be deported to some city just east of Wales that you'll almost—but never quite— recognize, and you'll never see her again."

Justin glared, but he zipped the case back up.

"Why are you doing this?" Lani asked. "You're part of Faerie too."

Robin laughed, a sound that got more troubling the more times one heard it. "Faerie is just a dream. And what is a dream with too many rules? As soon as you start putting limits on dreams, they become something else. Sometimes I just need to remind Orlaith, and all the others, with their pretty songs and dances, of that fact."

"Even if you burn everything down in the process?" Lani asked.

"Any life worth living has risks."

"We have enough risks, thanks." Megan said.

Robin was about to respond, when he was cut off by Cassia's fist smashing into his face, sending him tumbling. He sat up, rubbing his jaw. "Nice punch, Cass."

The satyress moved to follow up, but by the time she reached him, Robin had disappeared.

"I'm going to kill that son of a—" Cassia stomped the ground where he'd been.

"Later, Cassia," Lani said.

"I think I have working counter-magic now, maybe. I might be able to wake up Finn," Megan said, not sounding very sure, remembering what had been said about the strength of Robin's magic.

"But he still won't have the passes, and we're in a hurry," Lani said, "We need to get to An Teach Deiridh, now."

Chapter 25: Calling In

Despite the teens all jumping at shadows all the way to the correct park, the trip was uneventful. Megan finally ventured to ask, "Why isn't he throwing out another illusion now, or putting us to sleep?"

"Because as much as he doesn't want to believe it, Robin has rules too." Ashling responded as she started circling the mushroom ring to check the passage into Faerie.

"Such as?" Megan asked, looking around nervously.

"No cookies until after dinner, and do not meddle in the affairs of dragons," the pixie answered.

Cassia shook her head. "There's a reason faeries like him mess with lone travelers, or kidnap one kid, or maybe mess with a small group. He's powerful, but he's all tied up in his illusions. He casts one on five people, he needs to fool five people. He messes with the fair, he needs to fool 60,000 people. And when it starts breaking down, it backlashes on him. That's why he tried something subtler today."

"So, when we broke through his illusion before—wait, what are you calling subtle, the putting trolls to sleep, or the theft?"

"The part where he tried to magically mess with your mind, right before I hit him. You didn't think I did that just because I wanted to, right? I mean, yes, I wanted to deck him, but there was a good reason. And yes, when you figured out how to get through his illusion earlier, it weakened him a little. He'll be more careful, wait 'til we're alone, and *then* hit us hard with something."

"Comforting thought." Lani muttered.

"The path is ready." Ashling announced, stepping through.

Faerie, on the other side, was busier than any of the other times Megan had crossed into the realm. A unit of sidhe, and a handful of redcaps, backed up by a few others, patrolled the area around the gate, as if expecting someone else. Seeing a chance to travel in greater numbers, Cassia quickly indicated to the redcaps that she needed to go to the city to report.

"What's she doing?" Megan whispered to Lani.

Lani whispered back, "The passage to the Market is a long way, and traveling alone, we're in danger. In An Teach Deiridh, we can get some help."

"What kind of help?"

"Kerr kind of help. Maybe having some illusions of our own will help. And anything else we can get. Robin will definitely mess with us on the way."

"Can't we, you know, mention we have an idea, and get an escort or something?"

"Sure, if you want strings attached, or the risk of the Queen or Inwar interfering. Or maybe run into someone who'll sympathize with Robin. We need help, but we need help we can trust."

"But—" Megan began.

"But they're still faeries, Megan. Even when their world might end, they'll be true to their nature. We need to be more careful right now, not less."

Despite that, when Cassia indicated she had important information to report, others fell in to get them to the city quickly enough. Unfortunately, they learned, Riocard had stayed at the Market, though there were plenty of sprites more than willing to take news to him. Cassia remained with them to pass on what Robin had done with the gate, distracting the sprites while the teens and Ashling went to the kitchen that Kerr managed.

They entered to find a few members of Peadar's usual gang stocking up on supplies, while Peadar was talking to Kerr, who shifted about even more nervously than usual.

Lani was prepared to wait patiently for Kerr, staying well out of the way, but Megan, after a few moments of consideration, marched right up to the redcap.

"You want something?" Peadar asked, turning and glaring.

Megan let the march of inspiration play through her mind while not backing down, even looking directly at him. "I need you to do something for me."

"Kinda busy right now."

"You owe me."

"You're calling that in *now*?"

"Yep."

Peadar sighed. "What do you need?"

"Robin Goodfellow out of our hair."

"Great. Robin Freaking Goodfellow, on top of everything else."

"That's right, on top of everything else. And I'll even give you a head start. We're going to the Goblin Market. Somewhere along the way, he's going to mess with us."

"Not if we have a whole escort going with you, he won't." Peadar growled.

"No," Megan shook her head, "Then he'll mess with us later. That's not the deal. If you want the debt cleared, you and whatever buddies you need to take along deal with him for us, so we can deal with other things."

"And just how do you figure we're going to do that, huh?"

Megan smiled. "I'd love to say that that's your problem. I really would. But this is important, so I'll help you out. I remember how it goes. Pixies are good at finding somewheres. Sprites are good at finding somewhens. Specifically, interesting ones. So, we're pretty sure, if he thinks we're traveling alone, Robin will show up somewhere along our way to the Market, that'd be a pretty interesting when, right?"

Peadar considered that, looking around at some of his gang. "And I do this for you, debt cleared, and we go back to the way we were?"

"I know more than I did back then. And Justin still has the sword. But yes, no more debt for letting you guys off the hook. No hard feelings."

Peadar considered that, then nodded. "All right, but I still need to get these supplies off to other crews, and send word I ain't going to... well, where we were headed. But you got a deal. Get moving, we'll be along when you need us, and not a second before." He turned back to Kerr.

"One other question," Megan said, not flinching when the nightmare face turned back at her. "What's with the hat? The way it looks mortal-side, I mean. I get that it's convenient for it to be more... commercial, but is it just random or... for instance, are you really a '49ers fan?"

Peadar somehow grinned wider, in a way that didn't reach the yellow eyes. "I'm whatever you don't want me to be, Princess."

Chapter 26: Semper Paratus

Brownie work ethic conflicted with an obvious desire to be helpful, as Kerr apologized but explained that with all of the out-of-town visitors An Teach Deiridh was putting up for the duration of the market, the kitchen couldn't go unsupervised. They also learned that, unlike Robin's, Kerr's illusions wouldn't last long beyond their leaving the kitchens. Still, they arranged a bit of invisible cover to leave under, hoping it would buy them a little time as they headed for the passage to the Market. Kerr also gave them some homemade granola squares for the trip.

Ashling took the lead as they followed a twisting route through Faerie, sometimes on a path, often working their way through tall grasses and between fruit trees and berry bushes. While it seemed to Megan, at times, like there had to be a more direct route, or that Ashling might just be having fun with them, she'd traveled enough with Ashling to know that, whatever else she was, she was an excellent guide, and this route was almost certainly, somehow, faster than any other they could have taken.

Megan wasn't certain how long the full trip was supposed to take, but an hour into the journey, once they were well away from the staging grounds and the portal back to Fremont, a heavy fog rolled in. Megan started to sing up a whirling wind to drive it away, but found it hard to breathe. The others seemed to be having the same reactions. The Count was forced to the ground, while the cats both started coughing.

Justin drew the Sword of Light, and the fog parted away from him, forming a clear pocket, but only for a couple feet. The rest of the group closed in on him, and Megan started taking in the breath to open her song. The thick mist in the air might have muted the sound, but to their left, there was a loud crack, and the fog quickly began to dissipate.

"First Cassia, now you. Why is violence always your answer?" asked a smirking Robin, rubbing his chin.

Peadar, two other redcaps, a handful of sprites, and a single hag stood nearby, while more sprites moved between trees full of five or six different colors of apples. Peadar, club in hand, stepped forward. "Violence is never the answer. I got it wrong on purpose."

Robin eyed the crew in front of him. "So it's going to be like that, is it?" He gestured towards Megan and her friends. "Over them?" As he spoke, he was backing away, the smirk remained, with no hint of fear in his expression.

"It's going to be like that," Peadar said.

"Bring it, Boy Scout."

Megan blinked. "Did the blood-obsessed psycho with a baseball bat just get called a Boy Scout?"

"Yes," Lani replied, eyes fixed on the confrontation.

When Peadar lunged, Robin disappeared. "Damnit," the redcap swore, before looking to the hag. "You're certain he can't go far?"

The hag held up one hand and twisted a jet-black ring around on one finger. "I've hexed him so. He'll be near, but hiding," the huge woman croaked.

The sprites took wing at Peadar's gesture, gathering up like a flock, and sweeping out over the fields.

Megan was transfixed at the spectacle, watching dozens of sprites acting as one, with perfect coordination, the whole flight twisting and turning, before diving, trying to drive their quarry out of hiding, while the hag and redcaps sniffed around.

Lani tugged on Megan's sleeve. "We need to move now, while he's distracted."

"You don't think they'll get him?" Megan said.

"Whether they do or don't," Justin said, keeping the sword drawn and held out before him, leading the way, "We still have our own mission to fulfill."

Lani added, as they picked up their pace away from the confrontation, "And even if they do, I don't want to be alone in the middle of nowhere with either side."

"Good point," Megan agreed, picking up the pace, following Ashling.

It wasn't long before Megan started to get very tired. That was reasonable, in the long and winding walk. She tried to just keep trudging forward.

"Sleepy?" Ashling asked.

"Yeah," said Megan. "Long day already, and it wasn't that great a night."

"Yeah..." Ashling said slowly. "There's that. Hey, can you try to sing some of it off." Megan started in on the march, but the pixie shook her head. "Inspiration's not so much the thing right now. You need a stimulant. You know what might fit, magically? A little Sax & Violins. 'The One with the Complicated Rhyme Scheme.'"

Cassia smiled and happily sang along with Megan.

"You'll really want to try a villanelle.
If that's a pace you think that you can keep.
It's always worse than you at first can tell,
But if you want to ride a carousel
That's less of ponies than Victorian sheep,
You'll really want to try a villanelle."

Megan could feel how the patter of the words seemed to fall into place, to percolate in her mind like magical caffeine, but she tried not to overthink it. She didn't want to jinx anything when it was starting to work.

Somewhere between '*Though Dylan Thomas did it very well*' and '*The learning curve can be a little steep,*' was the sound of wings, a whole murmur of them, and a club swinging.

Despite their efforts to get ahead of the conflict, Robin seemed to be very motivated to slow them down. Now, as the gang came up behind them, the music provided an excellent soundtrack for a redcap attack on the small figure of Robin, who evaded their assaults with inhuman grace and quickness and disappeared again.

They continued walking, and soon Ashling wasn't bothering with her twists and turns anymore. They were just walking in straight lines. Megan was relieved, but she started being more observant about her surroundings—albeit observant in her own fashion, her eyes glancing from detail to detail to detail until she felt completely overwhelmed. But one feature, she quickly went back to—and then completely stopped in her tracks.

"Ashling," she said.

"What?" The Count circled back a little, since Megan had stopped, and flapped to hover in the air at conversational distance.

Megan pointed. "Does Faerie normally have what looks like dead pixels from an HD screen just hanging in the sky?"

Ashling looked. "Not *this* part of Faerie, no."

"Dreamscape illusion?"

"Dreamscape illusion."

Cassia groaned. "Should we muss Jude's goggles again?"

"We should probably just stand here a moment until we hear the—"

There was a solid 'whumph.'

The scenery shifted, and the chase was back on as the redcaps aggressively tried to run Robin down. Megan and her friends just tried to run.

Chapter 27: Up the Storm

Finally, they approached a hilltop, when Robin appeared again, this time holding a torch in each hand. The giggle sounded almost tired.

"Persistent and resourceful," he said. "This really might be a good show. Well, except that I've still agreed to do a job. So, something, something, fire, scarecrow." He dropped the torches, and fire swept down towards them, igniting the grasses.

"Is that an illusion?" Megan called.

"Do you want to risk it?" Lani shouted back.

Ashling jumped off of the Count's back, grabbing onto Megan's hair to keep herself balanced on a shoulder, and started humming. Megan had done more with winds, but knew the song. She hadn't practiced it a lot, but started into it anyway. As she did, it occurred to her precisely why she hadn't practiced it much. Quick, powerful gusts of wind she could do. Swirling winds she could handle. She'd even managed some small, personal rainstorms. This was something else entirely—not only calling up strong winds and rain, but trying to maintain control of all of it. Lani would say something about it having a lot of moving parts, or something.

Clouds gathered, and the wind picked up, blowing from behind Megan. It wasn't as focused as most of Megan's wind spells, but it didn't swirl, and she wasn't going for a single blast this time. Whatever Robin had that was driving the fires downhill instead of up and towards him, the winds disrupted it, and the fire's approach towards Megan and her group was blunted.

She struggled with notes and concentration on the song a couple of times, but Ashling kept coaching her, shouting in her ear over the winds and helping her along. The fires started climbing the hill, and spreading to the sides, though none of it touched Robin, parting and burning the grasses around him. Though blunted, the fires were still approaching Megan's group, and she knew she couldn't keep it up forever, or even for all that long.

Despite the difficulties, Megan sang louder, practically shouting the ancient lyrics to the skies, getting into even greater musical complexity. A couple of times, the winds shifted, but she kept managing to rein them back in, and within several seconds of her call to the skies, the rains started. It began as a drizzle, and then turned into a full torrent.

The fire was too intense already for the rains to put them out entirely, but as long as she kept singing, they didn't spread as fast.

Robin shouted something down to her from the hilltop, but she couldn't understand a word as she continued fighting to keep control of both the winds and the rain, even as she could feel the magical effort she was having to put into the song tiring her even faster.

That was when Peadar showed up again, charging up the hill towards Robin. Robin Goodfellow drew what appeared to be a wooden sword, and the two engaged in a fierce battle, Robin dancing among the fires to limit lines of approach, keeping the fight a one-on-one as the other redcaps and the hag continually shied away from risking the fires to go after him.

Somehow, the wooden sword took hits from the wicked club, and Peadar certainly seemed to take its threat seriously. As far as Megan could tell, Peadar was the better fighter, but any advantage that gained him was countered by Robin's reflexes, and the fact that Robin was fighting mostly defensively, just trying to stay out of easy reach.

They fenced and fought, with Megan continuing to call down the rains. Ashling had to hold on tight, frequently shouting into her ear to help Megan remember the words, and remember the music. Despite the help, and some practice, this was a stronger spell than Megan was used to, and a number of times, she felt like she was on the edge of losing control of it. If she did, she didn't know if the rains might stop, and a windstorm might whip the fires up, if a true storm might develop while they were in the open, or if it might simply stop. Her voice wavered, her throat grew raw, but as the flames died down under the rains, she started to rein it back in.

Without the fires, the redcaps started to close in on the fight, and Cassia charged up the hill to help, backed by Maxwell.

Exhausted, Megan staggered, almost falling before Lani caught her, and helped her remain standing.

As the crew surrounded him, Robin looked towards Megan, then at Peadar, and smirked once more. "Good fight, Boy Scout. Let's do it again some time." And he disappeared.

Megan expected more cussing from the redcap, but instead, he just looked her way, and nodded. It took her a moment, but she realized, given the lack of the effects of the redcap gaze, that he wasn't looking at her, but somewhere over her shoulder. She turned to look.

As she did, Robin reappeared, wooden sword in hand, readied to strike. "A lovely day, a lovely dance, Princess. I didn't want to do this, but..." He paused, as a tiny arrow grazed his arm, leaving a shallow cut. The arrow continued on, hitting the ground not far from Peadar. Robin paused, looking in the same direction as Megan, to see Gilroy, standing on an apple tree, bow in hand.

Peadar took the tiny arrow from the ground, placing it into his mouth like it was half a toothpick, point-first. The redcap grinned. "Tastes like rabbit."

"Oh come on, that barely drew blood!"

"Barely. Good to the last drop."

Robin glared, almost like a petulant child, as the redcap sampled his blood. Megan remembered, from that first chase, how that worked. Illusions, trickery, or no, the redcap would be able to follow that quarry flawlessly.

Robin Goodfellow clearly recognized the fact too, and he dropped the sword. "All right, all right, you've got me. I'm out." He reached into his pocket, pulled out far more black cloth than should have been able to fit in such a pocket, and tossed it at them. "I'm throwing in the towel. His mortal majesty can play this game alone."

Peadar nodded, and the hag turned her ring back the other way. Peadar made a shooing motion, "Very good. You may go now."

Megan would have thought what followed odd, had she not seen the Queen and King, after her aims last year had been thwarted. The petulance disappeared, and Robin bowed, deep and formal, to Peadar. "Well played, Boy Scout. Well played. Next time." And with that, he was gone.

Megan turned back to regard Peadar, but it was Lani who spoke. "So, what now?"

The redcap gestured back over his shoulder with one thumb. "The portal to the market is just up that way. There'll be guards from it any time now, coming to see what all of that was about. We're good?"

Megan took a deep breath, then nodded. "So long as he'll leave us alone now, your debt is paid."

Peadar grinned, waving to his crew, with Gilroy moving to settle on Peadar's shoulder. "Come on, boys and girls," Peadar called, "More fun another day. We have to go fishing."

Megan was pondering those words and putting the shroud in the pack when the Unseelie band reached them, and Peadar paused a few feet from her, ignoring Ashling's glares at Gilroy.

"One thing you and I can agree on, Highness: in the end, it always pays to be a team player," Peadar said, and then the group set off again.

Chapter 28: Clearance

True to Peadar's comment, various faeries coming from the Market showed up not long after the end of the fight, investigating the smoke. By then, Robin, as well as Peadar and his crew, had departed. Megan assumed whatever she'd interrupted with her calling-in of the debt had to be pretty important, because the Unseelie mob seemed in quite the hurry, once they'd verified that all was considered paid. Whatever the case, Ashling seemed a lot more relaxed once all of the sprites were out of sight.

The Market wasn't completely shut down when they got there, but some of the vendors were packing up their merchandise, and a few were taking down their tents. The oddity wasn't some of the dealers trying to get a head-start, it was what was left once a tent was removed. Instead of the usual small messes, or empty lots, once there was no longer a tent in place, it was like there was nothing there: small pockets of self-contained vacuum that Megan could only sort of absorb out of the corner of her peripheral vision, because any attempt to stare at any of them found her looking somewhere else. Eventually, the unoccupied space seemed to get smaller and smaller, until tents that had been a few spaces apart before were now neighbors. Megan didn't begin to comprehend how any of it actually worked, but Lani's comments—about how the market could appear and, when done, vanish—finally made sense.

"I wonder if there's any more edible hats left. Maybe they even have some closing down sales," Ashling said. "Some of the best are at a big purple tent that's smaller on the inside. No time to go see if they're still open, I guess."

"Smaller on the inside?" asked Megan, more than a bit hoarse, but feeling the need to ask. "Why would you do that?"

"Well, they cater to a more diminutive clientele. Sprites, pixies, brownie children, so on, so forth. Some of us feel much more comfortable when we can check out things just for us, without feeling loomed over."

"So why don't they just have a smaller tent?"

"At the price of this real estate?" Ashling threw her arms into the air. "You'd be stupid not to fill it up."

"I guess so." Megan had more questions, but her throat still hurt, and she still felt like she needed about a week's worth of sleep. "I just hope the map people haven't closed up yet."

"Cartographers," Lani said.

"They won't have," Ashling assured Megan, "With the weirdness of the market, and paths, once it's closed down, a lot of people need directions. Or want maps for the rest of their vacation. They do great business right at the end. Plus, there's the satisfaction part."

Megan hated to ask, but couldn't help herself. "Satisfaction part?"

Ashling nodded enthusiastically. "Goblins love telling people where to go."

Megan just sighed and accepted the water bottle Lani offered her while they walked.

True to the pixie's comments, the section of the market with most of the cartographers was still full. Megan noticed that in the adjoining area, where she'd spent most of her time when she'd had a chance to browse, the art dealers were mostly still open as well. It looked like a lot of the people buying full-sized paintings or statues were picking up their purchases now that they were getting ready to leave. She started to meander that way for a few last looks, but a tug on her shoulder from Lani reminded her that they were in a hurry and had more important business.

Megan drained the rest of the water, and followed. It took a while to find the correct shop. Not all of the shopkeepers were terribly willing to help competitors, while others were every bit as helpful, and verbose about it, as Ashling tended to be. Most of the latter weren't very helpful either. Finally, one goblin peered at the map and said "Go try Xurde."

The girls, the cats, the Count, and Justin followed his gestures to a large red tent, outside of which stood a woman with bright blue eyes and golden curls—her eyes were literally glowing with azure light, and her hair looked like actual coils of gold wire—

in clothes made of leaves and flower petals. The sign hung up on the front of the tent simply read "*Here Be Dragon*."

"Excuse me," Cassia said to the woman, smiling in a very Cassia fashion. "Are you Xurde?"

The woman blushed. Megan assumed that was what she was doing, at least. What it looked like was some unknown hand etch-a-sketching pink roses across the woman's cheeks as she smiled demurely.

"No," she said. "He's inside." She looked at the half-map Cassia was carrying. "That looks a little like his work, though. Let me show you in."

In contrast to the tent Ashling had described, this tent was far larger inside than out. It was as wide as the teahouse tent had been, but much more open, and was deeper and higher as well. A good third of the huge space was simply to accommodate the bulk of a brownish-red dragon, who lay on the far end of the tent, focusing most of his attention on writing on a map that was tiny compared to the creature, with a similarly miniscule stylus, clutched delicately between the tips of two claws. The booth had four more bright-eyed, golden-haired women, one of them laying on her front near the dragon, with a pile of maps in front of her, while she drew on the mostly complete-looking maps.

"So, a dragon who makes maps?" Megan whispered.

"With a little help," Ashling said.

"What's she doing?" Megan asked, as they approached.

"Drawing the bridges in. It's still a bit of a sore subject for some dragons," Ashling said.

That was all the whispering they got in, as the woman from the front announced them. The fact that she announced them as "Princess Megan and entourage" drew a smirk from Lani and a blush from Megan.

"Oh yes?" the dragon rumbled, looking up, squinting at the group. At first, Megan thought that smoke was rising from his nostrils when he spoke, until she studied the dissipating mist long enough to notice faint ice crystals in the breaths, disappearing not long after coming into contact with the warm air.

Megan did her best to curtsey, feeling like it was probably the appropriate gesture, though it felt awkward. Lani did it far better, and Justin, as usual, had no problem pulling off a very formal-looking bow.

The faeries and animals were less formal, though Ashling seemed quite pleased, waving enthusiastically. "Afternoon, Xurde." Megan wondered how she managed to pronounce the name so easily, but she was not going to ask and hear Ashling take five minutes to explain that obscure Spanish dialects are easy because they're so similar to Corvid.

"You seek a map? There is little time left, but perhaps something remains in stock. The girls can help you," the dragon suggested.

Megan was grateful, both for the sake of her voice, and so she could continue marveling at looking at a real, life dragon, when Lani stepped up to answer. "Actually, we need to see some records. We have half a map. We're trying to find out where the original was purchased from, and find out who it was that bought it."

"Show us the half-map," the dragon said.

Cassia drew out the torn map, holding it up.

Xurde was silent for several seconds, finally responding, "We sold that map. A very old one. Before my egg-time, even. It was not cheap."

"We figured out some of that. But we need to know who bought it, originally," Lani said.

The dragon turned his attention back to the map he was drawing, and one of the other girls spoke up. "I'm very sorry. We don't give away customer information. Store policy." As she spoke, Megan's heart fell. They'd come all this way, and it seemed like such a good idea.

Undaunted, Lani continued speaking to the dragon instead of the shop girl. "Oh, we don't want you to give it to us. We want to buy the information."

The dragon looked back up. "That's another matter entirely. What do you offer?"

Megan fished out the silver dollar, holding it up while Lani explained. "We need to look into your purchase records or something for the map. Find out who he was, what he paid, something."

Xurde looked to the girl who'd spoken about customer information, and nodded. She fetched a wooden box, opening it up to reveal three stacks of tattered, soiled $20 bills, bound together with twine.

"The guy paid in twenties at a place like this?" Megan asked, a little surprised.

"D.B. Cooper's lost ransom money is always welcome in this establishment," the woman explained. "It was sufficient to pay for *that* map."

Lani missed it, but Megan caught the emphasis the woman put on the word 'that'. "Wait, what do you mean that one? Just the half, and he paid for the other half with something else, or..." she interrupted.

"No," the woman explained, glancing at the dragon with a questioning gaze. Xurde studied the silver coin, when another of his hoard of girls held it up for him, then he nodded, apparently finding their payment sufficient for full disclosure. "The Cooper money paid for the marked map of the wights of Mag Tuired. This—" she dug to the bottom of the stack and pulled a folder from the box. She opened the folder and took a piece of paper from inside, showing a doctoral certificate for a Brian Angus O'Neill "— covered the payment for the map to Falias."

Chapter 29: Fal Stone

Once they verified that the cartographers had told them everything they knew about Dr. O'Neill, the group left the tent to discuss their next moves.

"Don't understand," Megan said a little hoarsely as they walked.

"Care to narrow it down?" Cassia asked.

"Why would one secret map cost a historic treasure stash, and one just cost a copy of his PhD papers?"

"Oh, I'm sure it didn't just cost the papers," Lani said. "Any more than that goblin doctor just had you sing a note once. Whatever academic career was based on that PhD has likely been eliminated from all human records."

Megan was trying to listen. She was. She'd taken her medication that morning and everything. But the morning was a long time before, and the emptiness-singularities of torn-down tents caught the corner of her eye more and more.

Ashling was just as bad when unable to verify for herself that her favored floral haberdasher was gone.

Lani noticed. "Cassia, why don't the five of you go check out the clothing section just in case? We'll go to the picnic area so Megan can have a snack and her meds."

While they were gone, Lani sat down with Megan on the grass and handed her another bottle of water. Megan drank, ate some granola, and took her multi-colored pills, wondering if doing so in the Market would affect things. Justin stood next to them. The sword wasn't in the instrument case, but he kept it in its sheath, at least, his hand still going to it occasionally as he kept a very careful eye out.

She was feeling ready to talk when Cassia, Ashling, and their boys returned. "So, I'm guessing Falias is sort of like Findias?"

"Sort of like it, yeah," Cassia agreed. "Except that where Findias used to be a place full of art, and music, and bright stuff, Falias started out all kinds of dark and gloomy."

"I thought you kind of liked that stuff?" Megan said.

"Violent dark, sure. But I'm not a real fan of necromancy. Undead just kind of ruin the party."

"So, it's full of undead things? Is that why you all left?"

Ashling made a number of attempts to clarify for Cassia, including covering the fact that party hats didn't help the festive spirit of skeletons and wights at all, and describing bits of the city, but Cassia interrupted again before she'd gotten off on too many tangents. "Once it got out of hand, sort of, but there had always been some nasty things there. The Sorcerer Kings of Falias were supposed to use all their dark power to make sure the restless dead stayed quiet and underground. Someone needed that kind of magic, so the Gods sort of put it in their hands. Records say that they actually did just that at one time, but in most of the stories the folks old enough to have lived there tell, occasionally those dark powers were put to use making wights police the city and walking bones deliver their tea.

"Okay, so that might explain the wights a little, if he has something to do with that. So he's trying to raise an undead army or something, you think?"

"Maybe," Cassia said. "Which would suck, but we've dealt with a few undead before."

"Or he could be trying to upgrade from Doctor," Ashling suggested.

"That whole line is either dead, or so diluted it doesn't matter," Cassia said.

"What whole line?" Megan asked.

Justin said "I think I understand. You're talking about the Lia Fail, right?"

Ashling pointed at Justin, putting one finger from her other hand on her nose, in a mixture of 'right on the nose' and obscene gesture. Megan was pretty sure the pixie would either claim it was an accident, or probably meant to simultaneously tell Justin he was right, while giving her opinion on O'Neill.

"What's the Lia Fail?" Megan asked.

Lani said "An artifact that was enchanted in Falias, hence, Fal Stone. Supposedly, when the true King of Ireland... or possibly

Scotland; there's been some debate... stands on it, it will sing or call out his name or something. But I thought that was in Ireland, where it was brought thousands of years ago."

"Unless one believes those Scots who say the Stone of Scone is the Lia Fail," said Justin. "Then England took it in the war, last I heard."

"Yeah, you're a little behind on that, Justin," Ashling said. "But the replica at Tara is better than the replica at Scone, I think. Even if they propped it upright where it's pretty hard to try to stand on. Doesn't matter, though. Brian Ard-Ri-Wannabe O'Neill needs the original."

"There were copies?" Justin asked.

"Well, yeah," Ashling said. "You think they were just going to leave the original mystical artifact around to get busted in half by 6th-Century temper tantrums or fouled up by 21st-Century vandals? That's why there was discrepancies in the legends and arguments as to which was the Lia Fail. Both are and neither is. But the one that does the singing is in Falias."

"That would do the singing, if the true Ard Ri ever stood on it," Cassia said. "But he won't, because after Daithi, there were no more. Not real ones, anyway."

"And an Ard Ri is...?" Megan was trying to keep everything straight.

"High King," Ashling answered.

"Okay." Megan thought for a moment. "...This might explain the 'mortal majesty' thing that Robin said. I mean, what if someone did have the right lineage?"

Lani nodded. "And with a well-connected last name like O'Neill...it's enough to worry about, at least."

"But what harm can actually being king be?" Megan asked.

"...well, the Ard Ri was what they call a sacred kingship." Ashling explained. Megan suspected there was something to what she was saying, because Cassia didn't interrupt her this time, on a topic Cassia obviously considered important. "Sure, he can't just show up and disband the government because he claims a rock sung when he tap danced on it. These days, people would laugh at him. But, see, then he'd call a lightning bolt on their heads, or have a giant serpent eat the laughing people. Because a lot of really ancient, really powerful things listen to the Sorcerer Kings if they know the right spells."

"Like wights and other undead things?" Megan asked.

"Well, those specific wights followed the Fomoire, so they were technically on the other side. But on general principle, sure," Ashling said. "Especially if he decided to rule from Falias."

"And you said sacred kingship. So, what Robin was saying about needing sacred things to wield sacred power...?"

"Yeah, he did say that, didn't he? Huh."

"He said it about the Balor-shrouds."

"Yeah."

"We're in trouble, aren't we?"

"We so are." Lani said.

Chapter 30: Gods and Monsters

They sat in silence for just a moment before Megan heard footsteps.

"If I may make a suggestion, dearest," said her father, as lightly as his rich, dark voice would allow, "You could use a rest. According to what I've heard from your chef friend and a few others, you've had a busy day."

"It's worse than they think, Dad." She told him everything. Ashling occasionally tried to out-talk her, but Lani would help steer things back when the pixie went overboard.

Megan's father listened to this all intently, jotting a few notes on a scrap of paper. "You definitely need some honey tea, a hot bath, and a good night's sleep. Ashling, Counts-to-18, please take this—" He handed the scrap of paper to the mounted pixie. "—to the Ballroom at An Teach Deiridh. Cassia, I would suggest you return to Fremont immediately and check on your friend the art model. Miss Kahale, Sir Justin, you'll probably want to join us as we get started on that honey tea." And Riocard started walking

"Okay, Dad, I just want to check," Megan said as she followed him to the tea stand. "Are you not talking about it because you don't think the guy who might have the wights might be trying to make himself king so he can have a zombie army, and he might be doing all kinds of weird stuff with Balor's shrouds so that he'll have something kinda-sorta-but-not-divine to draw his king-stuff from? Or are you not talking about it because you want to encourage random people to go King of the Zombies hunting?"

"I'm making suggestions in the hopes that you'll get out of here before the place closes, ask your mother if you can stay with Lani a few days—perfectly honest; I'm sure she's not going to leave your side when you go to Faerie—and get some rest before everything else gets started. I promise you, dearest, some of the least random people I know will be heavily involved. There'll be no stopping them."

"Like the Queen?" Megan asked as they arrived at the stand. And her father ordered the tea. "Won't she be all twitchy because Balor scarred her face?"

"Orlaith's experience at Mag Tuired was a little more complicated than that, dearest. Vanity hardly drives the pain of the memory so much as the... perhaps the best word is helplessness... of being one of the, essentially, 'junior varsity' players in a battle for everything, and suddenly being faced with the biggest, in every sense, of the gods' opposite numbers."

Megan listened and sipped her tea. "Did one look really burn off the general's arm?"

"And a very good wardenwood shield, as well," came a ringing voice from behind her. "Lost a fine wood spirit that day, among all the other casualties."

Megan nearly spilled her hot tea on herself. She was not entirely sure how long General Inwar had been standing there, looking down calmly, but clearly dressed to smite. Megan steadied her drink. "Um … Sorry your shieldghost died, General."

"Thank you. She knew her duty; she knew the stakes, and she knew the girl she was saving, if only a little."

"Oh. So... how'd you get the new arm?"

"Fortunately," Riocard said, "One of the smith gods—a fine fellow with whom I had the treat of a drink once or twice—was around long enough to make him an excellent prosthetic." He nodded to Inwar, who nodded in return.

"Pure silver, perfect articulation," Inwar agreed. "Let it not be said your gods never showed any appreciation for assistance, even if only the assistance of distraction while Lugh readied his spear."

Megan looked back and forth between them, eventually focusing on her father. "What was hanging out with a god like?"

"A good time. He was a minor god, more down-to-earth, sort of a very exalted working-class artist. But you should have seen his mother."

"Riocard certainly did." Inwar added.

"Tell me about her?" Megan asked.

The response surprised her, mostly in that her father didn't have a quick, casual answer. For a few moments, his eyes even looked unfocused, and his expression softened. "She looked at me, and then she was gone."

"Wait, you spent time with her son, but she hadn't looked at you before?" Megan said.

Riocard's eyes settled back on Megan. "To the Gods, at least the older set, the fae were often, well, how mortals see us. We helped them, certainly, and with a lot of ritual, or numbers, we can fulfill their roles now. Such as the dance now managing the turn of the more mystical side of the seasons. The Dagda, well, he used to handle that from his chair. Four notes on the harp, and worlds were in tune."

Inwar nodded, and for the first time, Megan saw some hint of similarity between her father and Inwar, at least in terms of their recollections of the gods. "A great deal changed when they left us to do their jobs."

Riocard smiled, but it didn't have the usual devil-may-care joy behind it, indeed, it was almost sad. "She left last of all of them, mourning and keening for her lost child. She walked across that bridge, and looked back once. I stood watch at the start of the bridge. She took one last look at the world, and then at me, and she smiled. And then she was gone."

"She didn't say anything, or..." Megan trailed off.

"She was in something of a hurry," Inwar said. "Leaving for the safety of the world and all."

Megan thought for a moment. "Wait, so if they'd already gotten all the remaining Fomoire frozen in a lake, why did they decide they had to leave?"

"Because we're talking about magic on a level of power where any barrier is permeable, when blood calls to blood," Riocard said. "And the blood of the gods and their enemies was so wrapped up, the ice would have melted in the back-and-forth charge. For the seal to hold, the gods had to find somewhere else to be."

Megan listened. "Is that why the ice is cracking? Because O'Neill is trying to do something with a kindasortanotreally god?"

Inwar raised an eyebrow. "We'll have to talk about that," he said. "Preferably tomorrow, on the way to Falias."

"We?" Megan asked. "So, you're not sending me home and getting me out of harm's way?" she asked, more than a little surprised.

Riocard shook his head. "You need to be there."

Justin finally spoke up. "You have far stronger forces, and she's been through a lot already."

Inwar and Riocard exchanged a glance, the General frowning, and Riocard looking more thoughtful. "Robin Goodfellow took time out of his busy schedule of knitting and arson," Riocard said. "I choose to believe that's not for nothing, and bring you along. But, of course, Sir Justin, she's going to need her knight."

"Then I'm coming too," Lani said.

"I had assumed as much, and will prepare suitable transport for all of you. But first, baths, and a night's rest. Ashling will fetch you in the morning."

Megan managed to convince her mother to let her stay at Lani's. Mrs. Kahale didn't care for the idea of the teens going along to the lost city but didn't argue with Riocard's judgment either. The family's good-nights were, Megan noted, much more lingering and extra-huggy than usual. That made sense. Just in case.

Justin laid out his chainmail for the morning, though he placed the hat with it. Despite the events of the day, as she settled in, thinking about going to war alongside the faeries, and storming a city of the undead, Megan was positive she'd never get to sleep. Five minutes later, exhaustion caught up with her.

Chapter 31: Mobilizing

Kerr had apparently been up all night. When Ashling brought Lani, Megan, and Justin to the castle, Cassia meeting them there, a spread was laid out of every breakfast food Megan could imagine and possibly a few she couldn't have.

"You'll want to make sure to have some of the cream-cheese-and-sea-salt eggs," the brownie said, scampering around the room. "And I've checked that the fruit is all human-safe, but the honey with the corncakes is local, so don't have much if you're allergic to pixie dust."

"Wait," Megan said, looking at Ashling as they all sat down to eat. "Pixie dust is a real thing?"

Ashling sighed. "Tinker Freaking Bell. Yes, pixie dust is a thing, but it'll only make you fly in the Timothy Leary sense."

Megan decided to have her corncakes without honey.

Everyone ate enthusiastically while Kerr continued scampering around grabbing packages. "Lani, your dad and the rest of the Corps of Engineers have taken all of my chocolate coffee shards, but there's powdered drinking chocolate if you want it. Oh! And oatmeal walnut raisin cookies for the road." The packages went into Lani's bag.

Walking out the doors and going from the brownie's kitchen to the mustering grounds for the armies was a shock. Megan stepped out into a swarm of color and the susurration of wings. The wall of rainbow colors banked and turned, then exploded into countless pixies out over the ranks of the Seelie army.

The next thing Megan's eyes settled on were the unicorns— four in all, moving at a run. It took several seconds of staring at the quartet, moving in unison, to realize that they were pulling a massive chariot, constructed of nearly perfectly white wood and trimmed with platinum. Orlaith stood tall in the front of the chariot, calling to her soldiers, while Inwar, two of the sidhe knights, and a sidhe female bearing a large tome watched over her.

The chariot circled around a section of flat ground, where troops were organizing into ranks. While some of the Seelie knights had horses, others rode giant stags or great cats, and a small group even sat astride pegasi. Ranks of fae armed with similar weapons, whether spears, swords, or bows, grouped into organized ranks, while each of the sorcerers was given two guards.

Then there was the battalion of tree-people. Megan had once made the mistakes of calling them 'dryads,' before being informed—more snootily than one tended to get even from the sidhe—that they weren't *Greek*, if Her Highness would be so kind. She'd spent months trying to pronounce Ghillie Dhu and still wasn't quite sure if it was closer to 'gillydoo' or 'gillyoo.' Green-haired people were signaling each other with birdcalls among the giant branches of the mobile birch-tree squad.

The knockers—Megan had been told they were mine-dwelling brownie-kin, and they looked it—were normally a lot friendlier, as much as the Seelie-Unseelie divide, which seemed to capture the feelings of about 80% of each court, would allow. Right now, though, they were busy working at artillery pieces. A dozen massive catapults were the most obvious weapons in the arsenal. Slightly smaller trebuchets and ballistae were being checked, and lined up for deployment. Megan couldn't help but notice that, as they worked, the knockers said not a word. Instead, now and then, they'd rap their hammers in quick rhythms against the metal pieces of the heavy weapons, and others would take note and occasionally shift what they were doing in response to the odd 'language.'

Kerr headed behind the artillery, where Mr. Kahale, who had apparently been repairing weapons the previous night, waved to them, with frantic reciprocation from Lani.

Interspersed among the ranks were gnome musicians and brownie bannermen, their instruments and flags attentively at their side as Orlaith and her General surveyed their troops.

Megan had seen, from the Halloween charge of the year before, how quickly the Unseelie could be mustered if something was made interesting enough. That seemed to be the case here, as more and more Unseelie were gathering around where her father, clad in his briarmail armor except for the masked helmet, stood atop a pedestal of ice. Next to him, a great bar had been hastily erected, manned by a number of leprechauns and the ones that looked like leprechauns—clurichauns, that was it—who were handing out mugs of something or other as quickly as fae gathered. The Unseelie King himself reached for one, the briars winding back to bare his hand. Despite their usual nature, no one was drinking, not even Cassia, who was standing between Riocard's podium and Finn the troll. Every four or five sprites, in their murmurs of white, brown, gray, and occasionally blue, were working together to hold a single mug aloft.

Finally, Megan saw her father raise his own mug, calling out to his troops in a vigorous toast.

"Drink up, my friends. Drink deep.
I'm a close friend of gluttony in its place.
We've much to be proud of, so why not?
Envy... greed... well, there's only so much to go around.
Lust? Well, lust goes without saying.
Today there is only one unpardonable sin,
And that's cowardice.
Shed blood, break bone, drive our enemies before us.
And if you die today,
I'll toast your deeds myself, over drinks...
And if you shed blood with me today, and live...
If you fight at my side, why then, my friends...
You may loot the bodies of the fallen,
And drink on their coin,
So we can toast their memories properly."

A rousing shout went up, and the horde drank as one, then smashed their mugs upon the ground. Riocard put two fingers to his lips and blew.

Where Megan expected a piercing whistle, there was no sound that she could hear—but moments later, howls answered from the nearest trees, before a pack of giant black wolves came racing towards him. Riocard leapt from the top of his pedestal, which crumbled as soon as his feet left it. He landed astride one of the wolves moments after two of the bunny-people had managed to get a saddle on it. Four others, two sidhe, two redcaps, pulled themselves onto wolves as well. Another cheer went up through the massed forces, and the mob started to move.

"Your ride is coming." Megan heard her father's voice call on the wind. Another gust of wind carried a lavish carpet to them, with Ashling and the Count riding on the front. The pixie waved to them frantically. Megan looked at the hovering carpet dubiously. "A flying carpet, seriously? Will this thing even hold us?"

Ashling smiled. "Your father traded for it back in his Steppenwolf phase. It will hold you."

"How do we control it?" asked Lani, walking around the carpet as if looking for instructions.

"Leave that to the Count." Ashling said.

"Wait, he's flying it?" Megan asked.

"Well duh, are you going to tell me you know more about flying than he does?"

Megan, Lani, and finally Justin climbed aboard, and the carpet rose steadily, then took off, keeping pace with the marching armies. From above, Megan could see the two sets of forces stretching far ahead and behind them, with the personal vanguards of Riocard and Orlaith leading the way, and the troops guarding all manner of siege machinery trailing.

"How long is this going to take?" Megan shouted to the pixie, to be heard over the din of battle songs being played below as the troops marched.

"With the Queen along at the height of Summer?" Ashling called back. "Not very long. You'll see."

Megan turned her attention to the Queen, watching for a while, but not seeing anything of note until they approached a wide stream. Despite the lack of a bridge over the moving water, the armies kept charging on. Orlaith gestured forward, and the sunlight on the water grew brighter. The Queen lifted her hand, and the glimmering light against the water started to rise, first forming a bridge of sunlight across the stream. Not content, the Queen gestured higher, and the bridge arched higher, and widened, until a bridge of light started at water's edge, and continued over the horizon.

Neither army slowed, racing onto the bridge at full speed. It held up under all of them, with the Queen chanting and holding a hand high as the armies marched north. Megan tried to look over the edge of the bridge, peering off the carpet, before she felt Ashling tugging on her shirt. "Don't do that."

"Why not? This is incredible!"

"Same reason you close your eyes going through the gates. Some of the places we're traveling through aren't places."

"Huh?"

"Falias is a *really* long way away, but she's going to get two entire armies there between sun up and sun down. Seven-league striders have nothing on the Queen in a hurry."

"Whoa."

"Yep. Just enjoy the ride."

Megan contented herself with watching the unicorns instead, managing to somehow never get bored with that, no matter how many other visual spectacles the marching armies presented. In watching the four of them, and the majestic chariot they pulled, she lost all track of time.

As such, she was staring right at Orlaith's chariot when the Queen faltered for a moment. The bridge started to glow less brightly as the Queen halted her chants and her hand drooped. Starting near the horizon, the bridge began to...unravel, the strands of light fraying and undoing themselves, pulling apart closer and closer sections of the bridge. Orlaith didn't seem to notice, staring straight ahead, her sunrise eyes open wide.

Inwar placed a hand on her shoulder, calling out the words she had been shouting. A moment later, Orlaith joined back in, and the bridge was restored. The trip lasted only a short time longer, before her chariot, Riocard's wolves, and then the rest of the vanguard left the bridge.

From above, pulling her gaze away from the fae armies, Megan finally looked ahead, as Lani tugged on her arm and gestured forward. Looming in the distance at the edge of the rocky plain was a whole city of forlorn-looking gray stone. Its walls towered, and its towers were fortified. In front of the city, and extending into the city gates and the open spaces of the city stood an army even larger than that the fae had gathered. Most appeared to be skeletons bearing spears, bows, and swords. Others appeared to be animate suits of armor. Along the walls stood more skeletal archers, and honor guards for bony figures in robes similar to the sorcerers among the fae.

Megan pointed down towards Orlaith, still trying to figure out what the problem was, after the show of power she'd seen. They had been expecting the undead, after all.

Megan looked to the woman—or, well, female entity, at least—who had fairly recently tried to bloodlessly conquer all of An Teach Deiridh just to keep its processes more organized. Orlaith of the Seelie Court was, in broad principle, literally the paragon of control. Now, shielded from the view of most by her small honor guard, she was shaking.

Megan hummed lightly, a small enchantment she'd learned to help gentle winds carry sound to her more effectively. Over the sound, she heard the words: "General, we can't. We can't do it. I thought we would be able to ... but he was ... he's..."

Inwar kept his hand on her shoulder, looking where the Queen did. "You don't have to. Nothing can make you do anything. We deal with one battle at a time."

Megan followed their gaze, past the armies, past the walls, to see a single flag waving from the top of a spire, bearing an image she'd seen before, on the golems at Findias. On a field of black, there was a single dark red eye.

Chapter 32: Ready and Aimed

After catching the exchange between the Queen and Inwar, Megan pointed towards her father and his command staff. Ashling, or perhaps the Count, steered the carpet towards them. Her father was issuing commands to his lieutenants, but Cassia immediately moved to meet them as the carpet lowered to near ground level.

"You ready to go to war?"

"I... I don't know. Where are you going to be?" Megan said, shouting to be heard.

"Charging, where else?"

Megan had about a dozen questions spring to her head at once, picking one out. "My dad's wolves there, are they supposed to be part of the Wild Hunt, or where did they come from?"

"Nope," Cassia said. "Perfectly normal Giant Wolves."

"Right, because that's a thing that's normal. So where are they, anyway?"

"Where are who? You managed to get two armies marching on short notice."

"Where are the crazy horned guy and his giant black-dog army? We got a name. We got middle name, even."

"They tried, but O'Neill is still defending himself against the Hunt. Somehow. Wannabe-sorcerer-kings sometimes aren't messing around."

"That doesn't sound good," Lani commented.

Cassia gestured to the opposing army. "I don't know what you're talking about. This looks like a great day!"

Riocard shouted in Gaelic, and Cassia pointed towards him. "That's my cue, but I think he wants to talk to you," she called, maneuvering the chariot back into the front ranks.

Riocard turned his attention to Megan, a fierce expression of wild joy on his face. "Are you ready, oh daughter of mine?"

Megan glanced at the back ranks with many of the archers and sorcerers. "Do you want us out of the way until you figure out why we're supposed to be here?"

Riocard laughed, "Why would I do that? You got to see our concert," he made a sweeping gesture with one hand, gesturing out into the field. "This is your concert hall. This is your audience. Sing for me." He paused, glancing over the group. "Sir Justin, I trust you to keep an eye on her, of course. And it wouldn't do for you to catch a random arrow, so..." he whistled, and a pair of three-foot tall, ruddy-skinned creatures stepped forward. Each began to inhale deeper and deeper, sucking in air. As they did, they grew larger, until the tiny creatures were some fifteen feet tall. They moved to flank the group.

"Our very own arrow-catchers!" Ashling clapped, before growing more sedate, waving to the two now-giants.

Riocard gestured once more, and a wind swirled around Megan. "That should carry your voice to the whole field, but give it a moment."

Riocard turned, moving to the forefront, and as if on cue, the musicians stopped. The shouting and banging and stomping quieted, and a hush fell over the field. All around in the rear ranks, archers readied their bows, but held. Megan could see the rows of skeletal archers on the tops of the walls doing the same.

Though some way off, an armored figure atop the walls still commanded immediate attention—not only because of the armor, but also the glowing green eyes, like the wights they'd fought before. The figure raised his sword and gestured, and a tremendous scraping noise followed from behind the walls, before a giant, bony claw curled around the top of the wall in an open area, then another. A draconic skull followed, peering over the wall, looking out on the battlefield.

The armored wight pulled himself onto the dragon's back from there, then gestured forward. Climbing at the command, the rest of the dragon's skeleton came to perch atop the city wall. The figure raised his off hand and closed his gauntlet into a fist, and, as one, the skeletal warriors readied their weapons. Then everything was still again, as each assembled force waited for the other to make the first move.

Orlaith provided that first move, lifting a hand. As she did, a blast of flame hurtled from the skies, disintegrating several of the skeletal warriors.

A moment later, hundreds of arrows were loosed, and then both sides charged. Megan closed her eyes and shied away from the flights of arrows. She heard the sound of dozens of them landing amidst the ranks of the fae, hitting rock, hitting wood, hitting the earth—but none hit her.

She finally dared to open her eyes, first seeing Justin standing before her, a white shield held high, and flaming sword at the ready. Both of the giant fae who had moved to flank her showed signs of having arrows stuck into their skin, but none of the wounds appeared terribly deep. Regaining confidence after the moment of panic, she started to sing. True to her father's words, the song rose above the din of battle, carrying out over the field.

One of the siege weapons, a giant trebuchet, was rolled up near her position, and Lani ran to help the crew. Ashling and the Count flew to Riocard's side. Justin held his post, and more fae rushed around her, joining the charge ahead into the opposing army.

The wight on dragonback gestured, and the skeletons moved with perfect coordination. Megan heard shouts warning of flanking maneuvers, and other things she didn't quite understand, and kept on singing the inspirational battle march. As she did, she found more and more of the musicians among the faeries picking up her tune, helping carry it even further.

Even in the mass chaos, Megan couldn't help but notice the leaders of the fae. Orlaith's chariot charged forward, steeds lowering their horns and battering aside the first of the opposition. Inwar had taken over the reins with one hand, holding his sword aloft in the other, shouting commands to the ranks that followed in his wake. A company of mounted knights followed, guarding the flanks of the chariot and helping to clear the way.

Orlaith launched more fire into the undead ranks, to great effect. Despite her efforts, and those of the knights, the chariot's charge stalled after crashing through the front ranks of the enemy.

Inwar held there, shouting commands, guiding the troops and holding ground.

Orlaith, however, apparently decided that wasn't enough. She rose from the chariot into the sky on wings of fire. Arrows shot her way turned to ash before they reached her, and from on high, she pelted the field with bursts of pure light, which disintegrated the first opponents they touched and sent a shockwave rippling out from the impact, scattering others.

Riocard, Cassia, and Riocard's fellow wolf-riders outdistanced most of their colleagues. A rank of skeletal pikemen set their weapons to receive the charge. Riocard surged ahead of the rest, laughing like a maniac. He drew his sword and waved a hand. When he reached the line of pikes, he maneuvered the wolf between them, and not a single skeleton moved to adjust. When Riocard's blade struck one, it shattered like ice. The Unseelie King's companions followed suit, destroying the frozen warriors.

Another gesture of Riocard's blade, and a wind, far beyond anything Megan could even think of singing up, blasted rows of skeletons out of the way.

In answer, the wight on dragonback gestured forward, and the skeletal dragon leapt from the walls to cut off the charge. What followed was a chaotic whirl. The wolves leapt and climbed, with the dragon tossing or batting them away as best it could. A swipe of a claw smashed Cassia's chariot, but the satyress rolled away from it just in time. Then she followed the now-loosed cats in trying to scale one foreleg.

The fae advanced, slowly smashing their way through the horde, leaving ruins in their wake. There were screams, blood, and injuries, but there was no question to Megan's eye who was winning the day. The numbers remained intimidating, but the fae seemed to take few lasting injuries from the mundane weapons, and the field was carpeted with the broken bones of the enemy. Megan sang louder still, inspired by the spectacle, and caught up in the rush of her first large-scale battle.

The fae's front ranks were nearing the gates, and Riocard's wolf had finally managed to leap into the midst of the dragon's empty ribcage, and was working on scaling higher to bear his master to where he could threaten the enemy commander directly.

Megan was just reaching the crescendo of her song when a bright red light flared from within the city. A moment later, a wave of crimson light radiated outward, passing through the walls and out over the field. As it did, the scene abruptly changed. Broken bones healed, and defeated skeletal warriors rose again, made anew. The fae who had rushed into their ranks were suddenly surrounded.

As that happened, reinforcements rushed out from the city gates—but these bore jet-black weapons of twisted and notched iron. They caught several of the faerie vanguard unprepared, as they'd turned to assess the threat of the rising warriors. When the new weapons struck, the wounds didn't heal, and dozens of fae—sidhe knights, fierce redcaps, monstrous trolls, and others—fell and didn't rise.

The lead wight's eyes flared brighter as the red wave reached it, and the dragon's eyes took on a greenish glow of their own.

The red light didn't merely invigorate the undead. Where it passed, many of the fae seemed to freeze in place, or turned and fled, under some powerful fear enchantment. Megan had spent the better part of a year growing used to the alien expressions on those various types of faces, whether nightmarish or inhumanly serene. Terror fit strangely on them.

In the skies above the field, Orlaith's next blast was answered by a green burst of fire from the walls. She didn't fall as it hit her, but the bright flames taking the form of wings at her back flickered. Another blast followed, as another of the missing wights, this one draped in a rotting beige sheet, cast at the Queen from the top of the walls.

Another salvo of arrows rained down from the castle walls. This time, where they struck, there were screams—some of them cut short. Amongst those screaming in pain were Megan's two faerie guardians. Justin held firm, but both of the giant faeries were staggering and quickly deflating.

The radiating light faded out before it reached Megan and the back ranks, but she was in enough of a panic without its help. Her song stopped, and Megan tried frantically to locate her father. She finally spotted him, thrown from his wolf as it fled in raw animal fear, leaving the King fallen on the ground before the dragon.

She lost sight of him again as the renewed front rank of the skeleton army began to advance.

Chapter 33: Under Fire

"My Lady, the music." Justin's voice cut through Megan's growing panic. Before he could say any more, the advancing ranks of the enemy army reached them. Justin went on the offensive, blocking an initial attack from a skeletal infantryman, then sweeping his sword low.

The instant the Claiomh Solais struck a skeleton, the sword flared brighter, and flames washed over the target. The enemy did not so much burn up, as simply seem to lose all animating force, collapsing in a pile of bones. He destroyed five within seconds, giving them a little more room. "Help them rally," he added.

Megan caught on, with the main threats being the cold iron arrowheads. She began to sing, not trying to layer on the rains this time, just calling up the best sweeping winds she could—at least without drawing on the song full of F#s—and directing the windstorm towards the walls.

The next salvo of arrows launched, and most flew backwards, or fell short, some even striking the other army's own ranks. Some of the archers and others on the walls were carried backwards. Despite the winds, those who still stood were already readying more arrows, having been given no other command.

Megan glanced back towards the dragon, quickly going from panicked to exulting to see the effect her bardic magics could have even on this scale. Where she'd struggled with the song before, flush with a momentary victory, and not needing to so tightly control the winds this time, she just sang louder. Justin was still killing skeletons in front of her. While one of her former fae guardians lay still, the other had pulled a couple of arrows out of himself and, despite terrible burns on a shoulder and a leg, was reinflating himself back to giant size, before stepping on another skeleton trying to reach her.

Confident that her watchers would hold, Megan's eyes moved back to the fight with the dragon. She saw her father surrounded by skeletal warriors, and the dragon was raising a claw.

Cassia was the nearest fae to him, but Megan wasn't sure if the satyress would reach Riocard in time to do him any good.

Riocard kicked back to his feet, narrowly avoiding attacks where he'd lain. His hands came together, then swept outward. Skeletons flew away from him in all directions, and when they struck the ground, they shattered into thousands of frozen pieces.

Free of the immediate assault, he noticed his sword lying on the ground. As he held out a hand, the sword flew back into his grip, even as the dragon stepped down. Cassia was still whirling and turning, her sword shattering bone and knocking opponents aside as she fought towards Riocard again, still not quite reaching him.

The undead dragon's foot came down, and Riocard held his free hand up. Instead of smashing her father, as Megan briefly expected, the foot stopped as soon as it hit the King's hand, like he'd caught it. He held like that for a moment, before Cassia reached him, and her sword-sweep hit the dragon's leg at the ankle. The foot shattered, and cracks ran up the massive legbones.

The pair fought a retreat away from the dragon before skeletal reinforcements caught up. As they did, others moved to reinforce them, including Cassia's cats and Riocard's wolf—the latter getting a glance from the King as if it had sorely disappointed him. Even so, as it reached him on the run, knocking aside more of the undead, Riocard swung back onto the creature's back, facing off with the dragon. Two of his original vanguard caught back up as well, moving to defend Riocard's flanks.

The din of battle picked up elsewhere as well. Inwar and his chariot were under full siege, but the general was still shouting orders, gesturing with his sword, and cutting down everything that came into reach. Others among the demoralized Seelie ranks, and even some of the Unseelie, responded to his call, cutting off their retreats or getting back into the fight, forming up to hold the ground they'd taken. Others moved forward from the back ranks to try to fight their way to Inwar, reinforcing the ranks and replacing the fallen. Throughout it all, Orlaith remained in the skies, engaging in a battle of sorcery with the wight on the walls.

Inwar shouted again, voice echoing out over the battlefield, and the next surge of reinforcements came. Orlaith wasn't alone in the air for long, as massive swarms of pixies and sprites blanketed the skies. They swept just above the field in a bright carpet of color, and where they passed, skeletons were tossed aside. Megan stopped the winds, trying to not disrupt the tiny fae, and started back into the fear-dispelling march instead, helping to restore morale to the shaken ranks.

The charge picked up again, Inwar rallying troops to him in a renewed push for the gates. With most of the field still in chaos, more and more of the fae moved to support Inwar's efforts, moving to engage the skeletons with the iron weapons, holding the gates against all comers.

Though the enemy archers shot down some of the tiny fliers, most of them reached the walls. Dozens of the skeletal bowmen were swept off of the walls in the charge, though those who approached the spellcaster atop the walls were met with flashes of greenish light, before being tossed away without reaching him or his immediate support.

Megan spotted a dark shape trailing the glimmers of pixies: Ashling and the Count circled about the field, gaining altitude, then diving. The winged fae dealt with many of the archers and finally attempted to sweep over the walls and enter the castle—but from the way they stopped in the air, they might as well have hit a glass wall. Some veered away in time, others hit the field hard. In the end, though, only a single dark figure made it through—and a few moments after he had flown right past the glimmers, the Count circled back around, trying to get back among those pixies that had dropped onto the city wall.

Within a few moments, Megan started to see the skeletons on the city wall drop their weapons and stumble into each other. Only a few fell off the walls, but in the meantime, the dropped and scattered pixies and sprites started to rise and rally

Inwar's charge stalled near the gates, but his efforts forced the enemy hand. The wight on dragonback shifted his attention from his direct battle with Riocard's company to guiding the forces holding the main entrance to the city.

Just as it appeared that the fae were gaining ground again, the red light built up, and surged out from the city again. The fallen dead rose once more, and the fae ranks wavered, though they held better than the previous time. The pixies and sprites scattered, multiple groups splitting off from the main body. The injured undead dragon began to heal, going back on the offensive against Riocard and his group.

Amidst this, the Count apparently found Ashling again. The pixie pulled herself back onto the crow, narrowly avoiding an attack, and leaving the wall behind, heading towards Riocard.

Seeing the pixie coming, Riocard gestured, a spiky wall of ice rising between himself and the dragon. The Count landed on his shoulder. Riocard shouted something, then Cassia shouted back. He responded, and, reluctantly, the satyress turned, smashing her way through the battlefield and heading back towards Megan and the back ranks, with Maxwell, Jude, and the pixie and crow close behind, leaving Riocard and his wolf-riders to face off with the tactician wight and his dragon.

Megan was then somewhat distracted, if not almost mesmerized, by the sorcerous battle on the walls. Orlaith erected a fiery barrier against the wight's next assault, and turned her attention on the forces below. Fire rained from the skies upon the ranks of undead nearest the gates. While the cold iron weapons were unharmed by the fae magic, the same couldn't be said for the weapon bearers. However, despite the power of the spells, the flames wouldn't pass beyond the open gateway, seeming to strike the same invisible, impenetrable barrier that the sprites and pixies had hit.

The wight on the walls seemed, in turn, to be taking advantage of this spare moment to ready something complex. His hands were spread wide, each glowing with green fire, sparks arcing back and forth over his head. There was a hitch in Megan's breath as she watched the sheer force of the charging energy.

And then something shattered the top of the parapet right in front of the wight, a puff of shards of stone filling the air. Not only did the wight's spell fizzle, but when the dust cleared, he'd been knocked to his knees by the impact. Orlaith's next strike kept him there, his own magical shields flickering under the assault.

Megan glanced back to see Lani standing atop the frame of a trebuchet, holding tight to a stack of papers, doubtless full of scribbled mathematical calculations taking wind speed into account, while looking like she might break into a victory dance. The artillery crew, however, just loaded another stone.

Justin drew Megan's attention back to closer matters with a shout of "Incoming!" Indeed, a dozen skeletons were rushing their position, spears lowered. Megan's song faltered a moment as she looked at the oncoming rush, and was still looking when Cassia's sword shattered one of their skulls from behind. Cassia and Justin engaged the skirmishing party as Megan gathered her wits and picked up the inspiring melody again, just as the Count, Ashling astride, rocketed right past Megan.

When the two fighters had cleared the field in front of her, and Justin was catching his breath, Megan finally paused again and looked expectantly to Cassia.

"Hey," Cassia said.

"Where did Ashling go?" Megan asked.

"She's getting Lani. You're all needed, Ric says." She was cut off before she could explain further by another assault group.

A few more broken bones later—all of these fortunately belonging to skeletons—Lani was there.

"Nice shot," Megan said.

"Aw, that's nothing," Lani said. "You should see the next one."

"No time," Cassia said.

Ashling settled onto Megan's shoulder to shout into her ear, "They're making a show of hitting the gates as a distraction. We need to go!"

"Huh? Go where? What even happened with you?"

"A dramatic roller coaster of emotional arcs—not to mention the physical arc off the Count's back; it should be recreated for Universal Studios. I'll happily tell you more about my complex experience of personal growth and how it should be franchised later, but it boils down to a couple of things. One is that that glimmer or no glimmer, the same trick that opens your window opens belts and bandoliers. More pressing is that there are some *amazing* wards against faeries covering all the inner wall trellises. So you're up!"

"So, just me, Lani, and Justin against whatever's in there?" Megan asked, feeling like that mostly meant Justin versus whatever O'Neill had planned, at the moment.

"Caw!"

"The Count says he should go," Ashling translated. "I'll keep an eye on your dad. He'll need the help."

"The boys are going too," Cassia said.

"Okay, so they're *not* faeries!" Megan realized too late that she might sound overexcited about having that matter addressed.

"Yeah. They're mixed. Part actual leopard," said Cassia, as if it were self-evident. Then she frowned again. "But if anything happens to them…"

"I believe," said Justin, "that as Megan's champion, I would be responsible for taking any thrashings merited, but, to be honest, if anything were to happen to the cats, I would probably not be in a position capable of standing to take said thrashing."

"Heh. Good point," said Cassia. "Be good, boys."

Chapter 34: Princess of Power

"There's way too much fighting up there, we'd never get through." Lani said.

"Which is precisely why Riocard is buying you time." Ashling answered cheerfully. "Ready for cookies?"

Megan and Lani both looked at the pixie, trying to parse the question without success. Finally, Ashling sighed. "You're not going in that way."

"I believe I understand," Justin said after a few more moments of thought. "This is the city of the dead, but also holds the King's stone. There's gates for kings, quiet doors for undertakers."

"So, there's just one exhaust port, hardly worth mentioning?" Lani asked.

"Oh, it will be guarded," Cassia said. "They're not going to be that dumb about it. But posting too many guards there would tell people where the hidden door is. We're going to get you to it."

"But if the walls are that warded, Ashling's guidance shouldn't work. How are we supposed to find a hidden door? The place is huge."

Cassia nodded. "There's actually a number of them. Ric knew where a couple were. He knew some of the undertakers, used to hang out and collect the occasional bookmark. He told me how to find one."

"Ok, but they're still going to see us coming. They've got people... ex-people... things on the walls all the way around." Megan said.

"No they won't. You're missing a very important part of 'we.'" Ashling said, gesturing the Count forward. The others followed further into the ranks towards some of the support staff, with Megan trying very hard to ignore the shouting and din of battle behind her as the red light renewed the enemy armies yet again.

Kerr met them amidst the support staff lines, bearing a plate of cookies. Kerr insisted they each take a few, before handing off the serving tray and letting a couple of other brownies help fit Kerr into a light armor vest, and a belt bearing a selection of cleavers and heavy knives.

"Wait," Lani said, as the armor was buckled into place, "You're a civilian."

Kerr shuffled a little, but finally gestured out towards the battlefield. "I don't think they care. Besides, you're an engineer, and you're going. I want to help my friends too."

Lani looked ready to protest further, but finally just nodded.

A new charge began from some of the reserves to draw attention as Kerr masked all nine of them with brownie illusions, and the group followed Cassia, circling around the faerie ranks and giving the battle a wide berth. It seemed to Megan to be taking far too long, but the only alternative she could think of would risk being caught up in the fight. When they'd cleared the main lines, they still passed skeletal patrol groups, some on foot, some on similarly skeletal horses or grouped with skeletal hounds.

Finally, they rounded one corner of the city walls, before travelling some distance along the side. Eventually, Cassia pointed to a spot on the wall with a patrol group staying near it. "There." she hissed.

The group moved quickly towards it, with Cassia explaining. "We'll take care of that bunch and draw attention. Figure out the hidden door and get inside. Kerr's illusion won't protect you once you pass the wards. Don't attack anything until you're in or they'll see you. Find O'Neill."

"And then force-feed him his organs, one by one," Ashling suggested, far too cheerily.

"Right, we'll... do something like that." Megan said, trying to focus on the door, and not the large group watching over it. Despite her worries, the illusion held, though Kerr seemed to be watching a couple of the skeletal animals on guard as nervously as Megan did.

The thought occurred to Megan that, over that much time, her father's memory might be faulty. She certainly didn't see a door in the wall. Before she could voice the concern, Cassia charged, rushing at the group. The first of the undead hounds shattered under the blow, and she was already on to the next. Kerr followed, somewhat less effectively, with Ashling shouting encouragement from the brownie's shoulder.

While the enemies were occupied, the teens and animals searched the wall, before Justin finally found a thin seam in the stone. "I think I found the door."

With the fight raging nearby, Lani still managed the concentration to figure out how to open the hidden passage. As soon as she pressed the right combination of bricks in the wall, a section of the wall slid open, if not quite as quietly as any of them would have liked.

Cassia, Kerr, and Ashling continued distracting and destroying the guards outside the walls, but more skeletal guards lay in wait inside the city, lifting their weapons when the door opened.

Justin and the cats led the charge through the door and into the city, while the girls and the Count followed behind. The sword proved just as effective this time, sweeping through everything in the way, skeletons collapsing if the sword so much as touched bone. Jude went low, taking the legs out from under a couple of the nearest attackers, while Maxwell feinted, drawing a swing and a miss from one skeleton before the cat pounced, knocking the undead warrior back into others.

Megan tried to keep her music quiet, going into her inspirational music to bolster Justin and the cat's efforts. It didn't feel like enough—especially when she was feeling like they needed to finish this quickly before reinforcements arrived.

Justin advanced into the ranks of the skeletal warriors, smashing down a couple more, leaving broken bones behind him. Once he did, Megan searched through the bones, drawing one of the swords, hoping to be able to possibly defend herself a little better. It felt odd in her hands, far heavier than she'd imagined. Still, she felt slightly better being armed, with so many skeletons, and all of the full fae left outside. The attempt at inspiration, being better armed, and her own shifting thoughts put her in minds of one of the stories of different types of bards Ashling told her. The Norse skalds still did the singing and inspiring but also helped with the charge.

The longer the fight dragged on, with Justin repeatedly forced onto the defensive, the more sure she was reinforcements would arrive any second. She was already rushing to help, wielding the sword in the closest approximation to Cassia's style as she could. She caught one skeleton entirely off guard, severing it at the spine as she moved to help Justin. Her first kill, or perhaps re-kill, with the blade convinced her to get more aggressive, try to help out more, and end the fight more quickly so they could move on. She was pretty sure Lani was saying something behind her but couldn't make it out over the fight.

Megan quickly regretted her aggressiveness when one of her swings deflected off a bit of rusted armor a skeleton still wore, and the flat of the blade struck Justin. He turned at the impact, reacting to a perceived attack, barely stopping himself from hitting her. As he did, one of the skeletons struck him. The blow didn't penetrate his chainmail but did knock him to one knee. With more warriors coming, he shoved Megan away, out of their reach, and did his best to defend himself under the assault.

After crippling one of his own skeletal opponents by shattering one leg, Jude came to the rescue, pouncing on one of Justin's attackers, though the cat took a both a cut to one flank as he turned, and then a glancing blow to the head as he attacked—which might have been worse had it not been for the helmet. Maxwell, having rushed into enemy ranks, used to fighting alongside Cassia, wasn't faring much better, bleeding from a dozen wounds, but still fighting.

More careful with her attacks this time, Megan looked for an opening, then lunged in with her borrowed sword again, shattering the skull of one skeleton. Lani found another fallen warrior's weapon and joined in. Neither girl had any practice with swords, but managed, so long as they caught busy attackers off-guard. As soon as that changed, and the skeletal warriors turned their attention to the girls, both quickly found themselves forced back, retreating from swings until Lani stumbled over a couple of broken bones and went down.

Megan took a deep breath. "Thistle, Lavender, Mulberry, and Mauve." The song developed into a burst of wind that caused the skeletons attacking her and Lani to stumble backwards. As Megan did her best to help Lani back to her feet, the skeletons recovered and advanced again, with a couple more joining them.

The two were backed up to the walls, fighting defensively. Megan managed to parry a sword blow, but found her sword trapped, even as another skeleton raised a spear. Before it could strike her, the skeleton's torso flew apart on impact from Justin's sword. In the time they'd divided the numbers, he'd managed to finish off those left facing off with him, and had rushed to help the non-combatants. He made short work of the attackers, and moved to help the cats destroy the last defenders.

"I think I'll stick with engineering. Unless I can bring a trebuchet next time," Lani said, dropping her sword.

"I don't know. That was kind of fun," Megan said. "Justin, could you teach me some sword moves?"

"Of course, my lady," Justin said.

"Okay, that's fine," Lani said. "But Megan?"

"Yes?"

"Until he does, maybe you should lay off the She-Ra act?"

Megan dropped the sword. "That might be for the best, yeah."

"Come on," Justin said, limping just a little as he headed deeper into the city, "Reinforcements will be coming soon, and we still need to figure out what O'Neill is doing."

Chapter 35: Hail

The group scrambled into a hiding place around the corner of a gray stone building just before the first skeletal patrol arrived. A pair of riders showed up first, soon joined by a crew of more typical skeletons.

"How many of these guys are there?" Megan asked in a whisper, peering out from around the building.

Lani tugged Megan back into hiding. "A lot, apparently. At least they're not individually all that tough. There's just a lot of them."

"Tough like iron golems?" Megan said.

"Or wights," Lani said. "I'm okay with there being just a few of those."

"If there are any more that aren't out on the battlefield, O'Neill will likely have them close at hand," Justin said. "From the inscription in the first tomb, we're missing at least one."

"So comforting," Megan answered.

The group started moving again as the literal skeleton crew left the site of the little skirmish and started checking the surrounding buildings. Trying to stay ahead of that patrol nearly ran the group into another. They were just able to wait until that patrol had passed, sneaking across a street to another alley before their pursuers found their hiding place. After that, they ducked into one of the larger buildings to get out of the streets, heading to the second floor to get a better view of the streets below.

"I can see at least three groups down there," Lani pointed out, after going room to room. "I'd have thought if he had this many more skeletons, O'Neill would have put them outside too."

"He doesn't need to as long as the army he has keeps getting back up." Megan said.

"And I'm starting to think he's just as worried about us as he is the fae army outside," Justin said.

"What exactly does he think we're going to do that the faeries won't, when they get a hold of him?" Megan asked.

"Walk right past the faerie wards," Lani said.

"Well, sure, but the pixies and sprites will undo those eventually, and they'll get in. Even with the skeletons getting back up, you saw Inwar. They were making progress. O'Neill can't think he's going to win like that, right?" Megan said.

"With so many resources held in reserve, carefully planned patrols, wards against the faeries," Justin said, "No, he doesn't think this army is going to win. He's studied the fae. He knows them too well. He's just delaying them."

"Okay, but delaying them for what?" Megan asked.

"I don't know," Lani said. "Something an Ard Ri wants to do."

"So you think he really is the Ard Ri?"

"I think it's likely he's likely gotten on the stone and proven himself, yeah, what with all the power. Like, y'know, necromancy."

"He's been doing necromancy already," Megan said. "He raised the wights."

Lani shook her head. "That's not necromancy. Wights are kind of self-starters. He just gave them a reason. But once he came to Falias, he could use the stone. And with the stone, and the right qualifications—bloodlines and body parts intact, mostly—he's the High King. And since High King trumps other kings, and Falias doesn't even have anyone else at the moment, boom: instant Sorcerer-King complete with necromancy."

"And an immediate skeleton army," Megan said.

"As a delaying tactic," Justin said again. "He's thinking bigger than just an army."

"Okay, so what's enough bigger than an army that you think it will stop the fae? He's made himself an awful lot of enemies," Lani said.

Megan glanced out the window and towards the highest tower. "Uhm, could Balor have been buried near here?"

"Well, no one know—wait, raising Balor? That's insane!" Lani said.

"Is it?" Megan said. "You saw the Queen. If someone had Balor on their side, they could control an awful lot, right?"

"Balor was on Balor's side," Lani said. "I mean, yes, in theory, but Balor isn't a weapon. He was a warlord with armies of his own. Some college professor isn't going to come along and be able to tell him to do anything."

"But he's not a college professor anymore, or he wouldn't be. If the stone says he's the rightful Ard Ri, that's got to be worth something, right?" Megan said.

"Balor fought the gods. What's a king in comparison?" Justin said.

"Okay, okay, so not controlling him. We'll assume for a second that he's not dumb enough to think he can do that." Megan said.

"Ashling would disagree," Lani said.

"Right, and maybe he is that dumb," Megan said, "But let's assume he isn't. What if he's not trying to control Balor, just trying to be important enough to make a deal with him?"

"What sort of deal?" Lani asked, sounding more like she thought the idea was plausible.

"Bringing him back from the dead would be pretty good leverage, to start with," Justin said. "O'Neill's obviously well informed. If he can make the deal in the process—which shouldn't be impossible to work out with necromancy—"

"—then there is his renewable source of 'sacred power, for a special value of sacred,'" Lani said. "And that would be why he wanted the shrouds. They're the only things that stop Balor's eye from just destroying everything he looks at."

"And you're just noting that now? I'm surprised you haven't planned for a Balor-raising since the point when we'd collected half of the things. You're supposed to be the reasonable one," Megan said.

"Right. I'm the reasonable one. Which is why I didn't figure on Balor-raising. Because if that's his plan, it's still completely insane!"

"Any other ideas?" Megan asked.

Lani was about to respond when the cats perked up their ears, and hissed a warning. "I think someone's downstairs. Out the window, and let's move," Lani said.

Megan was already hurrying for the window, checking to make sure the street was clear of patrols for the moment. "Move where?"

"Towards the center of the city," Justin said. "The Count is the only one who made it past the walls. So we need to get somewhere he recognizes and follow him from there."

"Caw!" the crow answered, flapping out into the streets ahead of the group as they escaped through the window, climbing down as best they could until it was safe to drop to street level again.

"I hope that means 'follow me,'" Megan said, "instead of 'this way to the smorgasbord.'"

The crow flew low, scouting ahead, and guiding them through the streets. Despite a couple of close calls, they managed to avoid any more fights. The closer they got to the center of the city, the more direct the crow's route became, as if he was in territory he was more familiar with from his fly-over. Finally, the sound of a voice, chanting in ancient Gaelic, came echoing through the alleys.

Interspersed between the verses of chantsong were occasional remarks, enunciated as if they were poetry, but generally along the lines of, "How much more can there be?" and "All right, maybe it is a little long for a Moment of Destiny, but it can still be an Hour of Triumph."

Avoiding another patrol, they circled around, trying to find an open path to keep moving towards the sound of the voice. The first two alleyways they found were blocked off by rows of skeletons, faced away from them, but still in the way. They finally entered one of the buildings bordering on the central square, moving until they could look through a rear window.

The window looked out on a massive, wide-open space, large enough for a good portion of a whole town's population to gather. Megan figured the place seemed well suited to making grand, kingly announcements, or for the whole populace to watch people either be declared Ard Ri, or humiliate themselves trying.

Despite the vast size of the central square, the entire east side of it was filled with one positively massive corpse. The titanic form, longer than a city block, stretched from one end of the square to the other. In sections, bare bone still showed, but over most of the body, organs and muscles were growing, spreading and stitching together over the skeleton. Familiar black cloth was secured over the face.

At the very center of the square, some fifteen yards from the giant's body, was a large stone, laid lengthwise. The entire length of the rock was decorated with ancient writing, which glowed, sometimes softly, sometimes brighter.

The man they'd seen in the Market before was dressed in far more lavish garb now—though Megan saw what Ashling had meant about a very fancy bronze lapel pin—with a sword at his belt, and a black-iron spear in one hand as he circled and paced around the center of the stone at the center of everything. As he moved, he shouted and chanted. The rise and fall of his voice seemed to be what was spurring on the reactions in the intensity of the glow from the runes.

Dozens of skeletons ringed the square, mostly blocking off the alleyways and easy routes to the ritual, and a large, armored figure with glowing green eyes stood near the stone, just far enough away as to not block O'Neill's pacing.

"We have to stop him," Megan hissed.

"There's too many skeletons out there, my lady," Justin said. "He's well prepared for us."

"We don't have a choice," Megan said, getting ready to go out the window. "We only have one shot at this." She paused, looking at Justin, "But, seeing as you have the sword and shield and stuff, you can go first if you want."

Justin nodded, then pulled himself out the window, with the others following. He quickly dispatched the handful of skeletons nearby, as the group rushed towards the ritual.

O'Neill glanced up and stopped chanting. "Your Highness is not much for protocol? It is not very decorous to enter someone else's realm without an invitation." He resumed chanting but changed his tone, calling out a different spell instead. Balor's body glowed a bright red, the same shade as the pulse they'd seen sweep out from the city before. The light exploded outward from the massive frame.

Justin thrust the sword up in front of himself, standing between the group and the oncoming light. The sword flashed brightly, and a part of the ring of red light dissipated, with the wave passing harmlessly around the group. O'Neill, for his part, looked infuriated but quickly calmed himself.

"Well," the man said. "I should at least reap the benefit of human company. Some historic moments should always be repeatable for an audience."

He stepped onto the stone, and Megan could swear he actually posed. It was debatable whether the cacophonous sound that followed was shouting, singing, or a heraldic call, but the words were clear: "Brian Angus Ui Niall, Ard Ri."

Chapter 36: Confrontation

Justin attempted to charge at O'Neill, but was cut off by the hulking figure of the wight. The Claiomh Solais survived the impact with the wight's claymore, but Justin was still sent reeling back.

"Your Highness should agree to work with me on my terms," O'Neill shouted to Megan over the sound of the swords clashing, and the rattle of the skeletons starting to move. "A little courtesy between royalty. I am the High King of Ireland, but that is just the beginning. You would like my Earth far better than living here under Balor."

"Just ignore him. Counter-magic," Lani hissed at Megan. She grabbed Megan's shoulder, trying to pull her back towards the wall, shouting towards O'Neill. "Give it up! Just let him stay dead. It's better for everyone!"

"Young lady, I have been planning this since you were in diapers. I think I know what is better." And the chanting began anew.

Justin tried and failed to get inside the wight's reach, but was slowly pushed back as well. In backing away, he did manage to cut down a few of the skeletons, but also took a couple blows that glanced off his armor in the process. Both cats moved to defend the girls, taking down the first skeletons to approach.

Megan took Lani's suggestion, launching into her reworked dirge of a countersong. She directed it first towards the nearest skeletons, no longer worried about drawing more attention. When she did, the nearest skeletons lost animation, tumbling into piles of bones.

"Very effective bardwork for not even being in the right key," O'Neill observed loudly between chant-verses. "I would still advise you not to be using amateur, jury-rigged magic during an undertaking of this caliber. You have no idea what I have studied and what I have sacrificed to reach this point."

"Not them, Balor!" Lani called, ignoring the sorcerer-king's attempt at professional feedback.

Megan shifted her focus there, trusting the others to guard her as she tried to counter O'Neil's resurrection spell. In response, O'Neill stopped his inadvertent monologuing and resumed his chants. Megan kept singing, feeling like something was pushing back against her spell. For the moment, Balor's regeneration froze, but the strain was building.

Used to Ashling on her shoulder, Megan was still surprised when she felt Lani lean in and try to sing in her ear. "Thistle! Lavender!"

Megan switched tunes. She had no idea why she was switching, considering how necessary the counterspell seemed to be, but not trusting Lani's judgment by now would be ridiculous. Eventually, she sang all the harder when she finally noticed the row of skeletal archers forming up.

The wind burst forth as the arrows were loosed. It was nearly too late, but the blast caught and scattered the arrows. Megan redirected her spell outward, not worrying about Justin so long as he held the sword. O'Neill also seemed to be protected, holding his ground—Megan noticed that, as the wind hit, the lapel pin's runes glowed brightly. Everything else caught up in the winds was affected. The wight staggered, giving Justin room to retreat further, cutting a path through skeletons towards the girls. The skeletons, much lighter than the wight, were far more than staggered. Many that weren't destroyed by Justin were knocked off their feet or crashed back into the rank behind them.

Megan almost picked up the pace, but Lani was pointing frantically at Balor. O'Neill's spell had picked up again, now unhindered by Megan's efforts, and the muscles were growing and spreading over the bones again. Worse, Megan could see a faint glow building up under the three secured shrouds.

Mrs. Chang's art class had once spent 20 minutes on a color called sinople, which was sometimes a dark red paint derived from an almost-black rock, and sometimes confused with green. As fascinating as such a visual concept was to try to grasp, Megan was fairly sure nothing was ever supposed to glow that color. And yet...

But Lani was calling out a dirge, trying to get her to focus. Megan switched keys and tone from the charged-wind song back to the counter-magic, with the resistance that came with it. She once again halted the progress in the resurrection, but was no longer able to help her friends.

The wight recovered his footing and came at Justin again, forcing the young knight to backpedal while fending off the bigger combatant with the Sword of Light. Maxwell went on the offensive, savaging one of the skeletons while it was trying to get back to its feet, and driving it back into some of the others, buying the group some room. Jude remained near Megan, doing his utmost to protect her from everything that came close, though he took a couple more wounds to his front shoulders in his efforts to do so.

Megan shifted her attention and her countersong to the skeletons pressing in on them, immediately feeling less resistance from O'Neill's magic. Several of the skeletons around Jude collapsed. So did a trio trying to strike at Justin while he focused on defending himself from the wight. She finally gave Maxwell a little bit of additional support—which the cat immediately used to rush to help Justin. Maxwell shattered a skeleton, driving it to the ground, and managed to bite down on one of the wight's elbows. Justin struck at the wight, but one of the skeletons got in the way, in its attempts to get in a strike of its own. The wight batted Maxwell away, sending the cat into a mass of skeletons, while Justin destroyed a few more. Free of the harassment, the pair clashed again, with the wight slowly driving Justin back towards the group.

By the time Megan looked back towards O'Neill, the regeneration had progressed significantly, and seemed to be picking up speed. She turned her attention back towards the ritual. This time it was even harder to battle against O'Neill's spell, as he directed his power against hers.

Worse, it didn't actually stop the regenerative process, this time, but just slowed it down significantly. Despite her best efforts, the muscles continued to knit, and in a few places, dead-white skin started to spread over the musculature. The bright impossible glow, muted by the shrouds, just grew impossibly brighter.

In the midst of the battle, O'Neill's lapel pin lit up again, tiny runes glowing across the bronze. Anger spread over his features, and he paused in his chants.

"Infuriating sideshow," he said, still managing to complain as if he were trying to do Shakespeare. "It will get them nothing. This would have been more efficient if I'd had more iron, but all is still well within the plan."

He shifted his focus, stamping one foot down on the Stone of Kings. The runes on the stone lit up, and the lapel pin's runes glowed brighter. Megan's mournful-sounding efforts showed signs of progress while she cast her magic without resistance. Some of the flesh and muscle retreated and shrank away from the massive body. All thoughts of continuing fled as the now-familiar red light started to build. Lani didn't even bother to try singing this time, just shouting into Megan's ear, "Morale!"

Megan shifted again, struggling to find the right notes for her courage-boosting song, starting off flat and off-tempo. The red light burst outward from Balor and O'Neill, washing over everything around. The skeletons Justin had destroyed remained broken, the sword apparently having destroyed whatever animating force enchanted them in the first place, but the others began to heal and rise again. The wight's green eyes blazed brighter, and he pressed his attack more aggressively. For a moment, Megan felt the fear spell trying to grip her mind, but neutralizing that effect was one of the first songs she'd learned. Her song bolstered her allies as well, and though Lani and Jude both froze for a moment, that moment passed.

The light continued out into the city, and, Megan knew, it would hit the armies outside as well. She could only guess that the pin was tied to the wards outside, perhaps both defense against magic in its own right, and an early warning system for when O'Neill's armies, or maybe his anti-faerie wards, needed refreshing.

When the spell had passed, with the rest of the fight still raging around them, Megan and O'Neill glanced at each other, like a pair of gunfighters about to draw. Megan started in again, trying to further unweave the magics O'Neill had cast on Balor's corpse.

O'Neill smiled and called upon another spell, flinging a blast of green flame towards her. Despite her counter-song, the fireball still exploded in front of Megan, diminished, but not harmless. She was flung back against Lani, and Lani hit the wall of the building behind them, hard. Jude was tossed back, rolling to a stop against the building as well. A dozen skeletons were blasted apart, and a few more tossed away, but more stepped over the bodies to take their places.

By the time Megan had shaken off the stars in front of her eyes from the impact, O'Neill was casting the spell to resurrect Balor again, while the archers had formed into ranks again, nocking arrows to finish them off.

Other movement attracted her gaze, just in time to see Justin, only a few feet away, blocking the wight's swing with his shield. This time, the shield broke, and from the scream, so did Justin's arm. The follow-through sent him backwards, hitting the ground just a couple feet in front of Megan, while Maxwell, bleeding from a dozen cuts himself, fought savagely to keep a trio of skeletons from closing in on the fallen knight. Megan sat up, looking back to Lani as if seeking a suggestion, but her best friend wasn't moving.

Chapter 37: The Man Who Would Be King

Megan seized on the first and most natural thing to come to mind. She called out the words to her storm song as loudly as she could manage, blasting skeletons and arrows away from her, and setting the wight staggering. Maxwell managed to dig claws into the cracks between the stones, and everyone else was on the ground. The loosed arrows deflected away.

O'Neill's head whipped around, looking at Megan as if she was a problem he had thought he'd already solved. The winds died down as she tried to switch to counter-magic, struggling to make the dramatic change so quickly. Thankfully, she didn't have to, as a missile of black feathers launched itself at O'Neill's face. The Count had picked his moment to disrupt the sorcerer. Green fire exploded nearby, sending O'Neill staggering and tripping over the stone, while the Count managed to fly away, though struggling to stay aloft and still smoking.

Megan was about to start her counter-magic again when she saw the wight coming at her, with no one in the way now. He raised the sword to lash down at her, and Megan froze. The swing missed, as Justin barreled into the wight's back, not quite knocking him off his feet, but managing to disrupt the swing.

Justin had his left arm, with half of the broken shield still tethered to it, cradled against his body, but still had the Claiomh Solais readied. The wight managed to turn enough to block the blow, but Justin's furious assault kept him off balance, staggering under the rain of sword attacks as Justin forced the undead warrior away from Megan.

Trying to set aside worry for Lani, and recover from the panic of seeing the wight coming at her, Megan picked her counter-magic back up, undoing more of O'Neill's resurrection magic while he was on the ground. As she did, both cats got back into the fight, moving to protect Lani and Justin from the skeletons as best they could, though neither was moving nearly as quickly as when the battle started.

O'Neill dragged himself back to his feet, snarling in Megan's direction.

"You had your chance. Now, I'll deliver your broken body to your father before Balor wipes out his armies," he spat, before launching back into the resurrection ritual. As he did, Megan met more and more resistance to her efforts, and the body began slowly healing once again. Still, it wasn't enough for O'Neill.

"Useless." he called, gesturing towards some of the skeletons between himself and Balor. A whole rank crumbled not simply to bones, but to dust. As they did, Megan could feel O'Neill pouring more magical power into the ritual, and Balor began to heal faster still. O'Neill chanted another guttural syllable, and more skeletons crumbled, their energies channeled into the resurrection spell, as he began overwhelming Megan's counter-magic.

Even more disturbing to Megan than watching helplessly as the giant body became more and more whole was the eye. The three shrouds still blocked a lot of the energy, but a few of the skeletons standing guard nearest the head disintegrated in the light radiating outward from under the shrouds. She tried to convince her mind it was imagining things when she thought she saw one of the giant hands twitching a bit on its own.

A moment of inspiration hit, and she found herself glancing around desperately towards the rooftops before finding what she was looking for. She nodded as she found it, holding up one hand, before tapping it to her chest, and finally pulled herself up on the wall.

"The only bodies he's going to find are yours and Balor's, and he won't know which is worse off," she shouted back at O'Neill. "Jude, help Justin!" she called, launching back into the counter-song, directing it again at the skeletons in front of her, de-animating a rank to buy herself and her protector a little room.

Just as the wight was finding his feet and trying to go back on offense, Jude crashed into one of his knees, while Maxwell continued protecting Justin, guarding the side the shield had been on. This time, Justin managed to evade the skeletons and cut right through one of the wight's arms. The wight released an unholy howl, the remnants of his arm catching fire—a fire which started to spread. Not dead yet, he swung his blade one-armed. Justin managed to get the Claiomh Solais in the way, preventing himself from being cut in two, but he was still launched backwards, landing hard on his injured arm several feet away, nearly losing his grip on his sword.

The wight started to follow up, but Jude held on, tearing at the wight's leg, slowing it down while the fires continued to spread. Jude finally let go and dodged out of the way of a wild, flailing swing by the wight. As soon as it was released, the flaming warrior lurched onto the battlefield aimlessly, swinging at everything in his path, hitting only skeletons, before finally falling and going still.

"Justin, the sword! I need it!" Megan called, before starting up on her countersong again. Justin fended off a couple blows from skeletons around him, hesitating to give up his best defense. In the end, he rolled away from his current attackers, despite the new surge of pain from his arm, and flung the blade towards Megan. It fell well short. He managed to come up with a leg bone in his fumbling for another weapon, desperately using the makeshift club to fend off the next attacks.

The leopards split up, Maxwell going back on the attack, trying to rescue Justin, while Jude charged the sword, pouncing on the skeleton nearest to where it had fallen. He took another wound, this time to a back leg, in his efforts to get his jaws around the hilt, but he managed, limping away from the assault and towards Megan, finally delivering the sword.

Picking the flaming blade up, she called, "Guard Lani," before she rushed onto the field, toppling a few more skeletons with her magic, heading for O'Neill.

She didn't make it far when O'Neill turned his attention back on her. "You can't stop me, child." he called, a few more skeletons disintegrating as he added their power to the ritual. The light from under the shrouds flared brighter, disintegrating whole ranks of the skeletons that had been guarding Balor's head. Worse, there was no doubt about it now: one of Balor's hands was shifting, and some of the muscles flexing. There were also skeletons coming at her from multiple directions, closing in, and there would be no one to protect her this time.

She picked up her song again, shouting the words to her counter-magic, and directing it not towards the ritual healing Balor, but O'Neill himself, and his protections.

Picking up on her shift in tactics, O'Neill called up another blast of fire. The greenish flame hit Megan directly, and exploded outward—but with the Claiomh Solais in hand, she weathered the blow with only minor burns. He lashed out again, with the same effect, and she moved another few steps forward, managing to destroy a skeleton by being just a little quicker on the stab than it was, grateful that all she had to do was touch it with the blade. "Now!" she shouted towards the rooftop.

The Count dove, unsteady in flight, but accurate enough to wrap his claws around the lapel pin, before tearing the shiny object away from O'Neill. He grabbed for the crow, but came away with just a few feathers in hand, as the crow climbed out of reach. Megan felt some of the resistance fall away as she attacked the protections around him, feeling some of them crumble.

She started to surge ahead again, drawing the skeletons, before shifting, and running towards Balor's body. O'Neill was still well protected by a dozen skeletons he'd left intact as a vanguard, but the eerie dark light seeping around the three shrouds, not even half of what were supposed to be there to stop the power of the Fomoire's eye, had ensured that that area was free of skeletons.

Megan dug into her pack as best she could, dragging out the neatly folded shrouds, holding them like a shield to cover herself as much as possible, until she could pull them over herself as a cloak, singing all the way, letting her voice build and build.

O'Neill's first spells failed to stop her, green fire both from his hands, and called down from the skies failing to get past the protection of the sword and the shrouds. He lunged for her, just as she reached the point she needed to in her building song. Megan didn't bother with controlling the winds, forgoing the verses that would help her direct it. Instead, she just trusted in the sword, and that her friends were some distance away, and let the wind go.

The powerful burst knocked pursuing skeletons away, and hit O'Neill in the back. Devoid of his protections, he stumbled towards her. As he grabbed for Megan, she ducked down, covering herself with the shrouds.

There was a flash of impossible light and a scream, then the sound of bones clattering around her as O'Neill's magics failed. Megan managed to avoid looking out, continuing to advance towards Balor with the shrouds protecting her. Her song switched back to the counter-magic, doing her best to undo the resurrection. By the time she was able to feel Balor's shoulder through the shroud, it was mostly bone again. Finding her way to the skull, she shifted the rest of the shrouds onto the first three, then, for good measure, hit the skull with the Claiomh Solais a couple times.

Getting all seven shrouds into place over the eye had stopped the effects, blocking it off, but Megan could still feel intense warmth through the magical cloths. She did her best to secure the last four shrouds, and finally turned to survey the scene.

The skeletons had all collapsed where they'd stood. The stone was no longer glowing. Justin and the cats had dragged themselves to the wall next to Lani, and the Count had settled in with them. Justin was looking her way, and trying to get back to his feet, with limited success. There were no more sounds of battle out beyond the city walls. The only sound, really, was the screaming.

Brian O'Neill, Ard Ri, was writhing on the ground nearby, showing signs of intense burns—though none as bad as the blackened stump where his right arm had been.

Chapter 38: Nobody

Megan hurried towards the others. "Is Lani okay?"

"Yes, she should be fine," Justin said as he stood unsteadily on his feet, his broken arm held close to his stomach. "Are you sure that you're—" He was suddenly muffled by Megan's lips against his. Once Megan managed to actually think about the kissing in progress, she decided she was strongly in favor of it.

Justin seemed to have come to a similar conclusion, frozen by the initial interruption and then going with it. Once they parted, he looked at her as if to say something, but didn't actually speak.

"Oh, Um, I hope that wasn't too..."

He shook his head. "Quite all right. More than all right. Not too anything. Let's talk about this. But let's look over Lani, and see if anyone's burns need anything."

"And a sling for your arm."

"And a sling for my arm. And bandaging the cats. And at some point we should probably confirm whether O'Neill is going to live."

"Okay, but, I mean, I promise I'm not trying to make a hostile chivalry environment here. If you don't want..."

"That's not the issue. My more prominent concern is understanding the pace of things. I've only just started studying for the GED."

"So you don't think you have time for a relationship?"

"I can always make time for you. I was thinking more in terms of not having money or land or family—beyond the Kahales, to whom I'm not formally entitled—or anything else to properly deal with the possibility of—"

"Okay. I get it. Justin, I can promise you, I have no intention of moving that fast. You don't need to plan for some kind of formal procedure for an immediate long-term relationship. This isn't courting, this is kissing. And saying let's try hamburgers as an actual maybe-date thing, or—" Megan raised a hand dramatically. "—if you can forgive the cheese, pizza."

Justin smiled, looking down slightly at his arm. "Megan, when it comes to you, I'm hardly going to worry about my health."

"What exactly do your 14th-Century sensibilities say about cheese on top of tomatoes, anyway?"

"My 14th-Century sensibilities are still having trouble with the concept of tomatoes."

Any further commentary was interrupted by the ringing voice of General Inwar, directing a few knights to secure the perimeter and engineers to prepare equipment for hazardous-materials transport. One of the menehune engineering corps, of course, made a brief digression to check on Lani, who insisted loudly that it might not even be a concussion.

As several trolls passed on the way to checking the shrouds, Megan heard a particular rich voice as well. She turned to see her father sporting a new necklace of dragon's-teeth.

"Everything's okay?" she asked.

"Of course everything's okay, dearest. You're fantastic, and we don't seem to have a Sorcerer-King on our hands." Riocard looked to O'Neill, who seemed to have caught enough breath, even after all his screaming, to try to hoarsely mutter some of the chants he'd done before. Nothing was happening. "Those powers were contingent on being king. There's a reason kings in the old stories lead from the front with their strong sword arms. The ancient rules don't look kindly on people without sword arms. So sorry." Riocard then looked to Inwar. "So it seems he's still alive."

"Easily remedied," Inwar said.

O'Neill didn't look panicked, actually giving Inwar a defiant look, at odds with the earlier screaming. He pushed his way with his good arm to sitting, and then stood, puffing his chest out and waiting for the death blow.

"Please don't," Megan said. "Getting killed at the end of a battle... that's something that happens to kings right? Not to disqualified losers."

The general actually smiled. "A reasonable point, Highness." The smile lapsed again. "Brian Angus O'Neill, for war crimes, for conspiracy with the enemy against the well-being of all realms—"

"Yes, yes, General, war crimes, I know," Riocard said. "Orlaith is understandably shocked by those, because dying isn't really a thing we do much around here. But it's still something that can happen in wars. I've started a few. And deals with ancient, undeniably evil beings? Not that unusual a by-product of grasping for great sorcerous power. Reaching for the glories of long dead ancestors... you know, O'Neill, I can respect that."

Riocard paused, tilting his head, looking thoughtful. "But I also know what you did in... what was it, graduate school? You pinned my scout to a butterfly board and broke her wings to steal her power. You denied one of my people her freedom... and that, I can never forgive. And so I pass judgment."

"Subject to Her Majesty's approval," Inwar interjected.

Riocard glared. "Yes, yes, I know what month it is, General. And she'll approve the living daylights out of this." He looked back to O'Neill. "I pass judgment. But what punishment? Oh what hells could I devise for you?"

Another pause, and a warm smile. "Several dozen, actually. But you're human, and American. I think there's a jury of peers thing, or similar nonsense. To save time, having already pronounced you guilty, I'm going to broadly paraphrase one of your fellow American mortals, then... thank you for sharing, by the way, Ashling..."

Riocard pressed his fingertips to O'Neill's temple. "With this touch, I give you this, Brian Angus O'Neill: every night, you shall dream of the glories of Faerie. You shall remember its peaks and valleys, its colors, its mystery. You shall recall, in vivid detail, the worlds, the realities beyond your own. You shall think in crowns and feasts and subjects and hunts for the white stag. It shall ever be in front of you..."

Yet another pause. "And you will never, ever find your way back. The paths shall fade, the memory of how to actually reach the realm shall always be just beyond your fingertips. As shall the names and faces of those who defeated you. So close, and yet..."

The Unseelie King gestured with flair. "I give you what all destroyers earn... nothing."

Riocard gave one more pause before he continued pleasantly. "Otherwise, you should heal up just fine, Dr. O'Neill. Oh, I'm sorry, all sales are final, aren't they? Mister O'Neill."

Chapter 39: Post-Carnage Brunch

Megan blinked awake, when rolling over or pulling blankets over her head would no longer shield her from the bright, golden sunlight streaming in through the windows. Even the attempts at careful placement of windows in the Unseelie wing of An Teach Deiridh did only so much to defy the light of Faerie at high Summer.

It took a few more moments to assure herself she wasn't dreaming, looking out over her room. Counting the meeting room, with its own table, couches and chairs, and several bookshelves, the suite her father had arranged for her was half the size of her house back in Seattle. King size didn't begin to describe the canopy bed, either. Lani had also slept in the bed—still was sleeping, in fact—and wasn't even in arm's reach. Jude had started the night curled up at the foot of the bed, some five feet away from Megan's feet, but had migrated over the course of the night to nestle against Lani for warmth. Ashling had her own satin pillow just over arm's length away on Megan's other side, while the Count had opted to rest atop the bust of Pallas set on a shelf near the door.

Aside from the massive canopy bed, empty bookshelves, a wardrobe, and a dresser with a mirror, the room was mostly bare and undecorated. Mostly.

Megan's first purchase from the market was mounted on the wall nearest the foot of the bed. She'd fallen asleep watching whirling leaves and swirling butterflies and rather liked the idea of waking to it regularly. Despite the difficulties caused by spending the card early, she was having trouble regretting the purchase now.

As Megan stirred, Jude did as well, stretching and yawning. That movement, in turn, woke Lani, who grumbled, and tried to push the cat away. She had no luck and ended up finally giving in and sitting up. Megan didn't think that Lani's eventually scritching Jude's chest was going to discourage future cat-snuggling.

"Morning," she mumbled towards Lani.

"Ow," Lani responded.

"You should get dressed," Ashling said. "There's a big breakfast being made for you guys."

"Br'k'fs?" Lani mumbled, still shaking off sleep.

"Shhhh," Ashling cautioned. "Don't say the 'K' word until you have pants on."

"Brownies, timing," Megan agreed, doing her best to move quickly despite lingering bruises and burns. As much as she'd have loved to have lounged around and not tested aching muscles, she was starving. They found spare clothes roughly in their sizes left in the dresser for them and headed into the receiving room before Megan finally said it.

"I hope Kerr will be able to join us for breakfast."

A few seconds later, there was a knock on the door.

Kerr didn't arrive alone, the breakfast feast requiring five brownies to transport everything, but Kerr was still happy to join them to help try and make a dent in all the food.

"So, I got to be part of the group who checked in on him," Ashling said. "You should have seen the look on O'Neill's face when he found them cleaning out an 'abandoned' office, seeing as how no one had ever heard of a Professor O'Neill."

Megan smiled, pushing a tray of honeyed fruit towards the pixie. "Professor who?"

"Shhhh," Ashling said. "I hear the BBC is looking for spin-off ideas. I'd hate to feed his ego like that."

The door opened again, this time with no knock, as Cassia entered, with Maxwell following. "Hey girls, hey traitor!" Cassia greeted them, scritching Jude cheerfully condemning his choice of sleeping arrangements. She dug into a couple of the meat options on the table with her bare hands, tossing the cats a share of breakfast, before making herself comfortable. "Nice job in there," she finally added.

"It was! You should have seen it!" Ashling said, "Especially the part where Megan charged on her Griffon. That was almost as cool as when Lani fired all three of her personal catapults."

Megan sighed. "Ashling, you weren't even there. And I don't have a griffon."

Ashling gestured accusingly at the Count. "You lied to me! How am I supposed to write down the official account of the battle for the war records if I can't trust you?"

"Caw, caw."

"Oh, well, all right then. Charged in on her unicorn!"

Megan was about to respond, then couldn't help but think of the four steeds drawing Orlaith's chariot, and decided that she could manage to wait for the official pixie account before passing judgment on the story.

Justin, now sporting a more elaborate arm brace and sling, and her father arrived not long after. Riocard had a book tucked partially under his arm. The archaic cover caught Megan's eye: *Mr. William Shakespeares Comedies, Histories, & Tragedies.* A place was marked in the book with what looked suspiciously like an academic certificate.

"Sorry to be late bringing your young man," her father said, apparently amused by the ensuing furious blushing from both Megan and Justin. "But I was catching up on some reading. Someone else's Midsummer nights."

"Where Robin Goodfellow is actually good for something?" Cassia managed to speak between bites.

"Now, now. Robin, as I understand it, dropped some very interesting hints. That counts as good for something, from a certain point of view. But best we all get fed now."

Thankfully, there was no shortage of breakfast, even at the rate Cassia was eating. Justin looked like he was about to say something to Megan a few times, but each time, decided it could wait.

Riocard waited until he'd properly settled in and filled his plate, then turned to Megan. "How did you enjoy your first night in your new room? Do you need anything else for it?"

"Well, I like it, but I'm not really moving in, you understand," Megan said. "Not full time. Mom's getting better. She's really... I don't want to miss out on that."

"Of course not, dearest. But there may be many different benefits to your mother's being able to enjoy herself again. At any rate, I don't think it need interfere with an occasional visit, and you'll want a place to keep those things that just wouldn't suit well under her roof."

"Good point." It was, but for the first time Megan could remember, she was feeling homesick. Last year, she'd pondered staying in Faerie, and never going back. It hadn't lasted long, but she'd had the thoughts a few times since. Now, real death and war had come to Faerie, while Megan couldn't wait to get to know the woman her mother was supposed to have been. She didn't doubt that she'd want to come back here soon, but despite the bed, and the feast, and the rest, she really wanted to go turn the radio on and make pancakes. As she looked towards Justin, she also found herself hoping pizza might happen soon.

The rest of breakfast went well, but by the time their magically repaired and cleaned clothing arrived, Megan was ready to head for the portal. Cassia and Ashling remained behind.

"We've got to get ready and go to a … thing." Ashling.

"Funerals," Cassia said more bluntly. "We're going to funerals. We've all got to remember how to *do* funerals. It's been a while. But you three should go home."

At the mention of funerals, Megan noticed, Kerr stopped eating. The brownie didn't say a word, or anything so obvious, but it spoke volumes. The last time there had been a fight, it was followed by a giant party and a lot of "No hard feelings." Her father'd also mentioned that grief wasn't his style. Megan wondered what Faerie grief was like, when it was in season, and she took Cassia's words for a warning.

Fremont still showed signs of the recent fair, with clean up in full swing. After all of the spectacle, and the quick shifts between realms, everything continued to feel a little unreal to Megan until they'd piled into *Space Ship!* and left Fremont behind.

Chapter 40: Someplace Like Home

"Hey, can you guys wait here for a second?" Megan asked, as Lani stopped in front of her house to drop her off.

"Sure, what do you need?" Lani said.

"Just... wait here a second. I'll be right back, as soon as I figure out if I can go through with this or not." She darted up the walk and headed into the house. She took a few minutes catching her breath, and working her nerve up, before calling, "Mom, can you come here for a minute?"

"What is it, sweetie?" As her mother approached, her face became more and more familiar, because she was getting worried. "Everything okay at Lani's?"

"Yeah. Oh, yeah," Megan said, desperate to get that new relaxed look back. "We had a great couple of days. I was just wanting to... maybe take the opportunity to introduce you more properly to Justin because they're in the driveway and ... and heandIarethinkingaboutmaybegoingout."

Sheila blinked. "Oh. Okay. Well...there'll be a lot to talk about, with that sort of thing. I guess we've never really needed to have that level of Talk before."

"Yeah. I understand. That later, maybe, and handshakes now?"

Her mother smiled. "Handshakes now sounds fine, Megan."

After both teens had hesitated after the kiss, Megan wasn't sure how Justin would handle this moment. For that matter, she wasn't sure how her mother would handle it, but it was suddenly very important to get the introduction of her maybe-boyfriend over with. To her relief, Justin handled it with perfect grace, certainly far better than Megan had handled racing over the introduction of the idea.

"A pleasure to meet you, Ma'am," he offered, stepping out of the car.

"I don't think, in all these months, I've ever heard your last name, Justin," her mother said with an awkward smile.

"Ludlow, Ma'am."

"Ah... like the port across the sound."

"I suppose so, Ma'am."

"Well, it's nice to finally be … formally introduced, Justin Ludlow. I certainly appreciate your and Lani's keeping Megan out of trouble."

Everyone laughed, and Megan hoped her mother wouldn't think that the girls laughed a little too much.

"I appreciate your daughter putting up with me," he answered.

After a few more idle pleasantries, Lani finally spoke up. "I'm really sorry, Ms. O'Reilly, but we have to be getting home." Megan knew that Lani's not having seen her own mother since her injury in the battle had something to do with that and nodded. They said goodbye, and Megan and her mother walked back into the house together.

"So how have you been?" Megan asked.

"Doing well. Erin from Sax & Violins called the other night to thank me again. I might need to get those girls in touch with some old friends of mine. They seem like they could get some use out of it, and they're all old enough I wouldn't have to worry about getting them mixed up in anything."

Megan noted to herself that her mother was still somewhat concerned with who got mixed up in what, but there wasn't the inherent anxiety in her voice, just matter-of-fact consideration.

"Makes sense," she said. "Speaking of connections, Mom, for my next psych appointment, what do you think about going back to that second-to-last clinic?" She'd already gone back to the old, moderate dosage for her ADHD medication, months ago. It would be nice to stop hiding that. "I kind of liked them."

Her mother pursed her lips, but only slightly. "They weren't too bad, I suppose. If you think your schoolwork could keep up just as well their way."

"I really think it could," Megan said. She tried not to sigh audibly with relief. The fewer secrets the better. Maybe eventually, if she was sure her mother could handle it, she could tell her everything she was.

"Okay, then we'll try it," Sheila said. "But Megan, with you maybe dating now, you know if you need to talk about anything..." she trailed off a little awkwardly.

"I know, Mom," Megan said, stepping up to hug her mother. "I promise I will. But Justin and I both really want to take things slowly. He's really old-fashioned. Like 'going out for pizza might be a little progressive' kind of old-fashioned. And I'm okay with that."

Megan's mother considered that a few moments, then nodded, still a bit hesitant. "All right, Megan. But school work comes first, right?"

"I'll keep my grades up. He even helps with my history. It will be okay, Mom, you can trust me."

Sheila hugged her back, not letting go for a few moments. When she spoke, it sounded like she was trying out words that she hadn't been expecting to say. "All right, Megan. I do trust you."

Megan took the win and tried to switch subjects again. "Can we try a little music together later?"

Sheila stepped back and smiled. "I have some work to get done later, after a couple phone calls, but if I catch up on everything, I think I'd like that."

"Phone calls? Not for work?"

"Not for work. A couple of old friends saw me up on stage. They want to know if I can come play with them on Friday night."

"Are you going to do it?"

"I don't know, Honey. There's a lot to do. And I'd have to leave before making dinner and things. They're playing an over-21 club, so I couldn't take you along."

"It's okay, Mom. I can handle dinner. You should go."

"You're sure?"

"Very sure. Go, have fun."

Sheila's smile became a lot more relaxed again, and she nodded. "Thanks, sweetie. I think I will."

Sheila disappeared to make her phone call, and Megan went up to her room. She put a Late to the Party CD on at a reasonable volume and didn't worry that her mother might panic if she heard.

Somewhere during "Psych Ward Composition," a tapping sound interspersed with the pulsing of the music. Megan eventually found the cause: Ashling was banging on the window.

The pixie made no preamble as Megan opened the window and the crow flew in. "So there we are, the Count and I, in the ballroom waiting for the King to be done being Professional with the Queen and the General. And that qa'hom Gilroy shows up."

"You and he got in a fight? Is that what this is about?"

"No, it's about what he said."

"Something rude?"

"No. He'd just come from the Fishing Hole. The cracks in the ice are worse, much worse, and they won't stop growing." Ashling took a breath. "The lake won't hold the Fomoire back a full year."

Book 3: A Fair Fight
Chapter 1: Underground

The will o' wisp provided the only illumination in the depths, the pale blue orb bobbing slowly ahead of the Gray Lady as she descended. Once she neared the underground river, blue light began to contrast with the pale greenish-yellow of bioluminescent fungus growing across the stone.

Two sentries bearing pikes with cold black iron at the ends crossed them in front of her path. "You're a long way from home."

The blue light drifted forward as the Lady stopped. "You should let me pass," came the whispering voice from the glowing orb.

"No one recognizes your authority here. Go home."

"I'm no longer seneschal, and I'm not here on the King's business. I will, however, have words with Tiernan."

The guards tensed, hands tightening on their spears. "Is that so?"

The Lady remained perfectly still, looking right past the pair. "It is so. He'll want to hear what I have to say."

The pair glanced between themselves, "Then pass your message along. We'll see that he gets it," the one who hadn't been speaking before offered.

"I will deliver the message to Tiernan myself. Tell the boatman."

The pair exchanged glances one more time, then the spears parted. "Tell the boatman yourself, and if Tiernan doesn't like what you have to say, it's your funeral."

"Perhaps so." She continued on to the water and lit the torch that signaled for a boat. The boatman hesitated, but gestured her aboard when she offered him two ring-shaped bits of metal. Tiernan did love his symbolism. And he could pretend he wasn't inspired by any foreign culture as long as the money was old and Irish.

The trip into the depths was a long one, and they passed three more guard stations along the only route, with dark-clad sorcerers and archers watching the passage.

A tall, especially pale young sidhe with wide, dark eyes and shock white hair—just one remaining streak a familiar shade of red—waited for her at the docks of the underground village. He was flanked by eight more warriors, bearing more of the long spears tipped with cold iron, holding them at the ready.

"How did you know where to find us?" he asked.

"I have my sources. You keep the pikes?" the wisp asked. "Here?" Despite the threat, the Gray Lady stepped off the boat.

"Any fight that happens with our own kind will be a real one," he said. "I'm more surprised that you're here. The middle of nowhere, a place that is barely a rumor as a den of 'renegades too far beyond the concept of order to qualify as criminal.' Something terrible could happen, and who would hear?"

As the wisp answered, "You would hear," the Gray Lady's pale lips parted.

A gesture from the white-haired man, and the pikes were all carefully raised to be less threatening, and all but one of the warriors, Tiernan's right-hand man, stepped away. "It'd be a real fight indeed. But it isn't necessary if you don't think it so."

The bane sidhe's lips closed again. "I do not."

Tiernan nodded. "Who sent you? My aunt? Her lapdog? I'd ask about your boss, but I hear that he kicked you out."

The Gray Lady narrowed her eyes slightly at mention of Riocard, but let the comment pass without any other note. "No one sent me. I'm on my own business."

"I'm not used to the King's hand having her own business. Is this something to do with the mortal?"

"The mortal was a tiny piece of something far larger. The ice is breaking."

Tiernan nodded. "So Balor wasn't all there was to it. I'd heard rumors, but Inwar, curse the Northerner, keeps things close."

"You knew of O'Neill's goals?"

"That he was going after Balor's grave? I make a point of knowing about those things that remind my dear aunt of her own mortality."

"And yet she stood against the undead."

"That was the undead. I'm curious what would have happened had Balor risen. And skeletons aren't Fomoire. Well, they shouldn't be. But they certainly exposed weaknesses in the vaunted armies of The Last Home, didn't they?"

"Perhaps. We'll know soon enough if they've dealt with those weaknesses or not."

"Not going to hold out hope for some saving grace, now that the experts in Summer and Winter are both on the problem?"

"I place very little stock in hope."

"Is that why the rumors can't sort out whether he fired you or you quit? Did you just cut your losses and run?"

There was another stretch of silence before the wisp spoke. "He has a daughter."

"Oh, yes. I know. I make it a point of hearing when my aunt has a plan sabotaged, too. I'm in favor, obviously, whether I've any regard for the Unseelie or not."

The blank-mirror eyes stared at him. "Are you?"

"I am."

"I would have suspected you might have approved of the queen's plan, assuming your obviously discreet sources reported it in full."

His dark eyes twitched. "They didn't need to. It was defeated by a mortal-raised child, so it was obvious that like most of her plans, it was based in high-minded intentions and no regard for reality." He waved dismissively. "And then, again, the matter with O'Neill. Lucky the girl was along, weren't they?"

"Do you really think Riocard has ever relied on something as uncertain as luck?"

Tiernan paused, narrowing his eyes. "You're sure you're not still working for the King? You sound like you still think much of him."

The Gray Lady faced Tiernan directly, so that he could look straight at her blankly-mirrored eyes, though the wisp continued to do the speaking. "I try to have a realistic assessment of the people around me."

Tiernan looked away, gritting his teeth, one hand curling into a fist, the other hand resting on his sword hilt. "You may wish to watch your words."

"You may wish to watch your temper before it gets you into trouble."

Tiernan relaxed slightly, hand moving away from the sword hilt, but only a small bit. "As long as we're talking about realistic assessments, Lady, what do you think the odds are that the Fomoire have kept your child alive, below the ice, all these years?" He finally lifted his eyes back to hers.

The Gray Lady tensed, and the will o'wisp darkened in shade slightly, staring back at Tiernan for several long, silent seconds, before she answered. "With these strange, growing cracks in the lake, we may find out before Midsummer, if the diplomatic efforts find no new solutions. They'll send messengers, and soon."

"Perhaps, or perhaps my aunt will be true to her word. Or perhaps she'll assume that we've already made some deal with the Fomoire. After all, they are the enemy of my enemy."

"And have you?"

Tiernan smiled. "Now we're getting to the heart of the matter." But he didn't say any more.

"In terms of the enemies of your enemy," the whispers resumed, "does hating the Ljosalfar, for instance, make people good neighbors?"

"They're still Northern savages," Tiernan said, waving dismissively. "But they've been mostly quiet ever since their last set of raids on the ogres. I'm not out to start wars, only to finish them. At any rate, be assured, Lady: if and when An Teach Deiridh sends messengers, we'll be ready and waiting for them."

Acknowledgements

We'd like to thank our spouses, Cody Armond and Jennifer Wolf, for their support, as well as our families: Bill, Carmen, Sam, Maggie, Ben, Jeanne, and Kiera Perkins, Gerry Cook, Carol Wells-Reed, Kelly and Scott Hendrix, and Matthew Lewis, who counts.

Thanks to the unnamable amount of friends and neighbors for sticking by us to this point. Thanks to Ben, Matt, Nils Visser, Leslie Conzatti, and Robert Black for their feedback, and to all those who read and reviewed.

Thanks to artists: Christopher Kovacs for the title page logo, Nikki Becklinger for encouragement in character exploration, and Shayna Walsh for providing some of the first Fair Folk Chronicles fan art.

Thanks to musicians: Jessica de Leon (alias Vicious Poppet) for providing promotional compositions, Kenneth Petrie and Ashley Hemm Petrie for answering random bardic questions, and Ryan Murray for assurances as to possibilities for upcoming audiobooks and on various other points. (And on audiobooks, thanks again, to Matthew Rose, Bobbie Hyde, and all those who've helped).

Thanks to authors: Lee French and the rest of the Clockwork Dragon authors' consortium for immeasurable support, the New Authors community, Seattle NaNoWriMo community, and the Writerpunk community for all the rallying.

Thanks as ever to the AFK Elixirs and Eatery in Renton, Washington, for being such a great venue for book events.

And thanks to everyone who bothered to read this far.

We hope you'll join us again in each of the Four Lost Cities, which are a story admittedly much older than ours.

www.clockworkdragon.com
www.punkwriters.com

About the Authors

Jeffrey Cook lives in Maple Valley, Washington, with his wife and three large dogs. He was born in Boulder, Colorado, but has lived all over the United States. He's the author of the *Dawn of Steam* trilogy of alternate-history/emergent Steampunk epistolary novels and of the YA Sci-fi thriller *Mina Cortez: From Bouquets to Bullets.* He's a founding contributing author of Writerpunk Press and has also contributed to a number of role-playing game books for Deep7 Press out of Seattle. When not reading, researching, or writing, Jeffrey enjoys role-playing games and watching football.

Katherine Perkins lives in Mobile, Alabama, with her husband and one extremely skittish cat. She was born in Lafayette, Louisiana, and will defend its cuisine on any field of honor. She is the editor of the *Dawn of Steam* series and serves as Jeff's co-author of various short stories, including those for the charity anthologies of Writerpunk Press. When not reading, researching, writing, or editing, she tries to remember what she was supposed to be doing.

72862989R00129

Made in the USA
Columbia, SC
06 September 2019